BUTIN

(The Rise of Russia's Fourth Reich)

Jason M. S. Wright

To the brave souls who gave their all for freedom.

TABLE OF CONTENTS

Chapter 1 1

Chapter 2 3

Chapter 3 8

Chapter 4 13

Chapter 5 20

Chapter 6 25

Chapter 7 30

Chapter 8 38

Chapter 9 45

Chapter 10 51

Chapter 11 56

Chapter 12 64

Chapter 13 72

Chapter 14 81

Chapter 15 86

Chapter 16 92

Chapter 17 96

Chapter 18 100

Chapter 19 106

Chapter 20 111

Chapter 21 117

Chapter 22 121

Chapter 23 130

Chapter 24 136

Chapter 25 140

Chapter 26 147

Chapter 27 154

Acknowledgement 159

About the Author 161

CHAPTER 1

The Kremlin's secretive behavior baffled Western pundits, intriguing them about the sudden rise to power of dictator Butin and Patriarch Onufry.

Both men materialized out of thin air. Their origin and importance appeared inexplicable. How did they rise to prominence, and where did they come from?

News agencies in Moscow said Butin's father died from wounds he suffered in the siege of Moscow or Leningrad, take your pick. Other stories abound.

Another story on the Net said his father was a Vlasov Nazi collaborator and displayed a photo from the British War Museum confirming the fact.

Early school records in St. Petersburg showed he came from Georgia.

The final official story states he was born in Leningrad in 1952 as Oleg Butin to a Russian couple alive until the late 1990s. However, a Georgian woman who passed away last year contradicted the story, claiming she was his mother.

Butin

What is the truth about Russia's leaders, vague as it is, and how did they come to power and create wars and misery that affected millions of people? Can one unravel the avalanche of misinformation without access to the Kremlin's archives?

Russian doctrine states that propaganda must contain 5% truth to make a lie believable. We can reconstruct the truth from the thousands of lies on the Net because each lie has a smidgeon of truth, and while lies change, the truth within them does not.

Our reconstruction of thousands of propaganda reports reveals the rise of dictator Oleg Butin and Patriarch Onufry began in the chaos of WWII and its aftermath.

CHAPTER 2

Vadim Ledkin came from Saratov, where many inhabitants were Volga Germans and Ukrainians.

He was twenty years old, a handsome man with a medium build, dark brown hair, and hazel eyes. Although he was a Russian, he spoke the local German dialect and Ukrainian.

He became a Red Army soldier in 1938, one year before Stalin and Hitler invaded Poland, initiating WWII. The two dictators were close allies and, in 1938, readied their troops for the territorial conquest of Poland.

The combined Soviet and Nazi forces overpowered the Polish resistance in a few days early in September of 1939, and the two armies met in Brest to celebrate their joint victory in a military parade on the 22nd of the same month.

The invasion meant to divide Europe between Germany and the USSR, with Russians occupying the eastern half of Poland, previously a part of free Ukraine established by the Paris Accord of 1919.

The Soviets began to clear the conquered territory of Polish transplants imported to the area from western Poland after the partitioning of Ukrainian lands by its neighbors in 1921.

The Poles were brought into the region to Polonize the territory by wresting it from the indigenous Ukrainians living there since the fifth century. To reverse the Polonization, Stalin issued an order to cleanse the territory of the Polish immigrants and anti-communists by shipping them to the slave labor camps in Siberia.

Vadim and two Russian soldiers came to the house of Adam Zebrak, a Polish American who emigrated to Poland-occupied Ukraine after WWI, where he bought land and settled in the village of his Ukrainian spouse.

The old couple came from New York City, where he was born, and his emigrant wife worked for over twenty years.

The owners were ill and not able to handle their property. They needed assistance to manage the estate and have someone to take care of them.

They decided to adopt Olena, their niece, who, along with her husband Denys, would oversee the farming operations and look after them. In return, she would inherit the farm.

Olena's sister Kaska and her spouse Petro lived in the same settlement. She was jealous of her sibling being chosen as the heir. Hoping to replace her as the inheritor by ridding herself of the competition, she informed the invading Russians that Denys opposed communism.

The Bolsheviks considered all land owners bourgeois or *Kulaks*, the oppressors of the proletariat, and would ship all of them to Siberian Taiga.

However, there was no point in deporting the old couple since they were unfit for work, but Denys and his wife were prime candidates as forced laborers.

Vadim entered the estate, shot its three guard dogs, and told Denys that he was on the list of men suspected of anti-Russian sentiment. He instructed the family to hitch up a wagon, take their belongings, and go to the railway station, where they would board a train to be deported as subversives.

At first, Denys thought the Communists came only to punish him, and if he fled, they would pursue him and leave his wife and children alone. Denys was an expert horseman and could ride like the wind.

When he brought the horse from the stall, he jumped on its back and took off. The Russians shot after him but missed. He stopped on a hill to see if they would give chase, but they ignored him and started packing up his family. Seeing his effort was futile, he surrendered and joined them.

Butin

Olena was crying, not knowing what was happening. She had no idea why they were deported and where they would be taken.

Hearing her laments, Vadim, who understood Ukrainian, took pity on her and told her to pack only warm clothing and flour and not bother with anything else because where she was going, it was cold enough to freeze the piss as it hit the ground.

Denys' father heard of the deportations and came to the station to bid his son and daughter-in-law goodbye. He pleaded with them to leave the baby boy behind.

"Olena, please let me have Vasyl. Don't take him to his death in the wilderness," but she would not part with the child.

The occupiers jammed thirty people into each cattle railway car without heat or a toilet. They locked the wagons and sent them to the Siberian Taiga. Some victims died on the way, and two-thirds perished later in Siberia within the first year and a half.

Having sent off the deportees, Vadim came to see the informant, Kaska. He led her to the barn and started taking off his pants as she cried and begged for mercy.

"Come here bitch, and do not scream, or I will cut your throat. You sent your sister and her children to their deaths, no doubt, to inherit this place, but none of you will own it because the property will become a collective where you will work like slaves. That will be your reward for greed."

Fucking greedy capitalists, he spat when he left her.

Vadim settled into a comfortable life of an occupier and raped Kaska again, but his tranquil life was about to change because the Nazis would invade the USSR.

CHAPTER 3

Stalin adored his German ally, thinking he and the Fuhrer would rule divided Europe as they agreed in 1938. However, the territorial ambitions of the Nazi leader extended far beyond the European continent. He had his eye on world conquest and had no use for the communists and what he termed the Slavic sub-humans.

Generals Zhukov and Tymoshenko tried to persuade the Russian dictator that Hitler would attack Russia. Instead of taking their advice, Stalin grew furious at their suggestion and threatened to hang both for implying his buddy would betray him.

To Stalin's surprise, the Nazis launched an assault against the Red Army on June 22, 1941. Russia's military fell apart in the first two weeks of the conflict. The Germans took over 5 million Soviet captives, and Vadim was among them. Overwhelmed, his unit surrendered two days after the initial Nazi blitz.

In response to the German invasion, Stalin became arrogant and refused to admit his losses or abide by the Geneva Convention. He disowned the Soviet POWs, saying there was no such thing as Russian prisoners, implying they should have fought to the death, and as far as he cared, they did not exist.

The soldiers resented the abandonment but could do nothing about it. The result of the arrogance was grim. Three out of five Soviet prisoners starved in German captivity.

The rest would meet the same fate, except their fortune changed when the Germans captured General Vlasov, the defender of Moscow and Leningrad during their siege.

Vlasov despised Stalin's attitude toward the Soviet prisoners. To punish Stalin, he offered to help Germany overthrow Stalin by forming the Russian Liberation Army out of the surviving Russian POWs to fight alongside the Nazis.

Vlasov reasoned that before communists, German czars ruled Russia for centuries, so why not reestablish a Russian monarchy advised by the German chancellor?

After he discussed the situation with Hitler, Vlasov agreed the USSR should be run by a czar-like figure, with Vlasov as the monarch, guided by the Fuhrer. Thus, Vlasov created the million-strong Army composed of Russian volunteers from the prisoners Stalin disowned.

Vadim joined the collaborators and wound up again in the same estate where he raped Kaska, but his victim was not there. The Nazis shipped her to Germany to serve as a slave laborer helping Hitler's war effort.

The war turned in favor of the Soviets early in 1943 when the 1st Ukrainian Army under Zhukov and the 2nd Ukrainian Army led by Konev pushed back the Nazi war machine at Stalingrad.

The Allies defeated the Third Reich in 1945, together with Vlasov's Liberation Army, which suffered its final defeat at River Oder. After the surrender, the soldiers of the Vlasov army became fugitives from the vindictive Stalin. The NKVD began to hunt for Vlasovites, whom they executed as soon as they found them.

The West aided the Russians in the carnage by handing them along with other collaborators to the Russian military police.

The Soviet authorities insisted all the slave laborers should return to Russia, but they were not permitted to force them to go back against their will.

The Allies rounded up the displaced East Europeans in internment centers, readying them to be shipped back to their homeland.

Although the communists forced many DPs to resettle in the USSR, some lucky ones migrated to Britain seeking asylum, and some managed to find jobs and stay in Germany as Kaska did.

The Volga Germans, repatriated by Hitler, were exempt from deportation and remained in the fatherland. Familiar with Germans and their language, Vadim saved his life disguised as a Folks Deutch refugee.

The authorities took him to a temporary camp in eastern Germany, where he met Zelda Gruber, a woman of German origin from Soviet Georgia. The two decided to live together as a couple.

To disguise he was a Vlasovite, Vadim assumed her name, and as ethnic Germans, he and his wife settled as farmhands on a government-run estate near Suhl.

Life was hard on the farm but isolated and tranquil until fourteen years later when Vadim took a job in a grocery store in the nearby town to better his family income.

The move was a fatal mistake because former slave laborers frequented the food market. Among them was Kaska. She recognized Vadim and reported to the NKVD that he was an imposter, a Vlasovite.

The KGB verified his identity and identified Kaska as the spouse of a dead Ukrainian partisan.

They came to Gruber's house at three in the morning and hung him, staging the murder as a suicide.

Butin

The usual Russian procedure was to kill all witnesses, and they would have, including Zelda's eight-year-old boy Oleg, but the commander spared their lives.

He sent Kaska to Siberia, Zelda back to the Georgian SSR, and the child to Leningrad, where a Russian family of Igor Butin adopted him.

Not knowing the Russian language, Oleg made up stories about his origin since he did not want to be labeled as the son of a German woman from Georgia and a Vlasovite father.

He informed his schoolmaster he was a Georgian, and his biological father defended Moscow from Hitler and died of cancer a year after Oleg was born.

He learned Russian and excelled at schoolwork and playing chess. His scholarly achievement drew the attention of the secret police that recruited him to study at the Red Banner Institute for Russian spies.

Upon graduation, the KGB stationed him in Dresden, Germany, near where he once lived and went to school.

CHAPTER 4

Denys and Olena Shpot sat in the boxcar on top of their two sacks of flour with their daughter beside them and the baby in her arms. They rationed their three loaves of rye and hoped it would last until they reached their destination. To guard their provisions, they took turns to relieve themselves in one corner of the wagon people designated as the bathroom. The stench was horrific, and people huddled together for body warmth.

They transferred to a different train in Kyiv and had a chance to stretch. The guards parceled half a loaf of bread for each adult and a quarter per child for the rest of their journey. The box cars were no longer locked. There was no place to run. The wilderness was all they saw from their confinement.

They disembarked at an old prison camp built over a hundred and fifty years ago by Ukrainians deported there by the czars to toil at the nearby salt mine. The name of their encampment meant *Sorcery*. It was about 20 kilometers from a railhead and 400 km from the nearest town called Serov.

They knew they were close to the Arctic Circle because the sun's rim poked just above the horizon on the day of the Latin Christmas. Vadim saved them from the cold and starvation because the warm clothing and flour proved essential to their survival.

The log dwellings were sturdy though ancient and were infested with ticks. Furthermore, lice of every sort plagued their bodies. The Communists had one rule. Fulfill your daily work quota and receive half a kilogram of bread. If you did not, you got less to eat. Nobody forced you to labor, but if you did not, then you received no food. The edict decimated the people. If they were weak or sick, they starved.

Olena's job was as a forest laborer. She had to score the bark of coniferous trees to make the sap flow into the vessels below. Using a sharp pike, she cut a long groove along the length of the trunk and made secondary V grooves feeding the central one. A collecting cup was fixed at the bottom of the groove.

The Russians called this tree-scoring method the American Way. Previously, one side of the tree was debarked, and the naked area was scraped for the pitch a while later.

The forest was so dense people got lost, some never to be found. They would call out to each other every few minutes to make sure they were within hearing distance of one another to prevent straying too far into the Taiga.

The job was back-breaking. Many people exhausted from work soon succumbed to lower rations. The kids were the first to die. A cart made rounds every morning collecting the dead.

The settlement had a crew of men and women in charge of the stables and children's daycare for the working parents. There were no Russian children. Local people refused to bring them into this destitute society.

The Russians of the region spoke a version of the language like Ukrainian. Most of them were descendants of the Ukrainians deported to Siberia by the czars.

Olena worked hard every day to meet her norm to secure her ration. During summertime, walking from work, she collected blueberries and dried them to feed the family through the coming winter. She hung a pail from her elbow while picking the berries. Blood ran along her arm from the bites by swarms of mosquitoes.

The first spring, the authorities supplemented their rations with potatoes. Denys dug up a patch of ground where his wife planted potato eyes, which produced a bucketful of spuds in the fall.

Denys did not work in the forest. The camp had no veterinarian, and Denys knew all about horses and became the de facto horse doctor. The commissar gave him a pair of yearling animals and told him to transport barrels full of tree resin to the railhead. On his way back, he would bring the empty containers and the camp's rations.

His life as a cart driver was hard, though eventful. On his way to the railroad, he would drive past the shackled prisoners as they marched from the Gulag to the mine. All had long beards and would squat beside the road as the armed guards counted them to check that none escaped.

He often got off the cart on a sandy stretch of the road to help his young horses pull the wagon because they were not quite grown. He loved horses and wanted to spare them from overexertion. Whenever he could, he got handfuls of oats to feed them. By the time they were two years old, they were the best pair of animals in the camp.

Once, along the road, a Gulag fugitive came out of the forest to meet him.

He asked in the name of Christ to please let him have something to eat. He did not threaten Denys, who had only his piece of rye loaf. He gave the man his ration and watched him disappear into the woods. Soon, guards with dogs appeared and asked if he saw the runaway. He said he did not.

The guards moved on. Afterward, he heard two shots. He feared the fugitive might have told the soldiers where he got the bread. If he did, the guards would imprison Denys for aiding the man. Helping an escaped prisoner meant a capital offense in Russia.

Sometimes, another wagon with pitch would accompany him. On one such occasion, a Polish teamster beat his hoses to make them get through the sandy piece of the road. One whipped horse succumbed to exhaustion. The Pole was in a dire predicament because the commander would condemn him to the Gulag for destroying government property.

Denys felt sorry for the driver and decided to help him avoid going to prison. He did this by telling the official that the man had a great quality wool coat for sale at a low price. The official understood the bribe, took the jacket, and falsely stated that the animal died of old age. Bribery was prevalent within the communist system.

On another occasion, his Ukrainian friend, Moroz, was the companion teamster. While the railway workers transferred the pitch from the barrels into rail tank cars, they sat for a cup of boiled water. His buddy took his coat off to relieve himself, only to find out one of the loading crew stole it. Without it, he would freeze.

He asked Denys to take his axe and follow him to where the crew rested during a break. He told him to kill anyone who resisted and not hesitate. When they came to the group, Moroz recognized his coat. He kicked the Russian in the face and reclaimed his jacket while Denys raised his ax in case someone objected.

Another time, on the way back from the station, Denys had a passenger. The man was a high-ranking commissar of the district. The powerful commander managed the region like an absolute dictator. They stopped along the way beside a cemetery to pee.

"Look at all those graves of your Ukrainian Cossacks dumped here by Catherine the Great," said the commissar.

The graveyard stretched for kilometers, farther than anyone saw from the road.

"Millions of your countrymen are buried in Siberia. Some brought axes they used to build the shacks you live in. The lucky ones died from the cold within the first six months."

On the way, the commissar fell asleep. His cheek started turning white from frostbite. Embarrassed, he did not know what to do. How would he face his subordinates for such an obvious blunder? Denys took a bottle of vodka from the provision for the local overseer and rubbed the frostbitten face to bring it back to life to save his reputation.

A year and a half after they arrived at *Sorcery*, Denys noticed a piece of seal meat wrapped in a newspaper. The word WAR appeared on the parcel, and as he unwrapped the paper, he read the headline. Hitler attacked the USSR. One week later,

all the young Russians disappeared. They left for the front.

CHAPTER 5

Hitler's invasion of the USSR changed the lives of the imprisoned population. The camp administrator said all Poles would be shipped South to Persia because of the agreement exiled Polish General Anders made with Churchill and Stalin. After the German attack, Russia became England's ally, as did Poland since it was allied with Britain.

The interned Poles were permitted to leave so their men could form a contingent of the British Eighth Army to face Rommel in North Africa. The women and children of the soldiers would be taken to safety in southern India or Kenya.

The Poles would head south to the Central Asian Soviet Republics and then across the Caspian Sea to Pahlavi, Persia.

Denys wanted his family to flee with the Polish transplants, but the commandant said he belonged in Russia since they were Ukrainians. Where did they think they were going?

Instead, the commissar of *Sorcery* asked Denys to go to the Russian front to bring back horses they needed for work at the camp. Denys would not leave his family to fetch horses from the conflict area and decided to escape.

He gathered his kids and his wife in the middle of the night and headed for the river with assistance from his friend Moroz. They untied a boat and put the family belongings in it. The current would take them downstream to the rail station. Olena, baby Vasyl in her arms, and daughter Ania walked along the bank. Denys lit a cigarette she could see from the shore as she followed the boat while Moroz bailed the leaky vessel.

Stealing the boat, a government property, amounted to a death sentence, but Denys fleeing for his life with his family did not care. Moroz helped Denys escape, but he would not leave with him. He secured the boat and went back to the camp. He told the commissar the poorly tied boat became loose and drifted away.

Moroz would remain in *Sorcery* with his lifelong Jewish friend Mandel. Both survived for nearly two years and thought they could survive for the next three years when they would be allowed to return to Ukraine.

Denys and his family mingled among the Poles as though they were Polish transplants and got on a train to Chelyabinsk. To feed the family, Denys sold his sheepskin coat for two kilograms of tea at the bazaar.

Russians drank boiled water and pretended it was Chay, so tea was a prized commodity. Denys divided it into small portions and traded them for food along the way South.

Butin

The family arrived at a settlement in Frunze, Kyrgyzstan, where Denys thought he might flee to China and embarked with a friend trying to find a way to reach the Chinese border. The landscape of the featureless grassland looked the same in every direction. The two got lost but found their way back and gave up on their idea.

Denys decided to risk disguising himself as a Pole and moved the family west to Samarkand in Uzbekistan, where they joined a group of Polish people.

The Poles were free to leave, but the authorities had no intention of feeding them, and many starved in Central Asia.

Olena had a sack of flour she used to feed herself, her kids, and two starving women housed with her. One named Aniela was a young single Polish woman whose entire family died in Siberia.

In Samarkand, the men were separated from their families to join the Polish part of the Eight Army. From a camp in Krasnovodsk Turkmenistan, they boarded a ship bound for Pahlavi, Persia, then to Iraq, where they secured petrol dumps to supply gasoline to the British forces in Palestine. They trained for combat in Egypt to confront Rommel in Cyrenaica and Tobruk, Libya.

Before they were allowed to leave, the NKVD made regular rounds to check identification papers to ensure only Polish citizens left Russia. The fugitive, Denys, had no ID.

The police arrested him, and two Russian soldiers marched him toward the railway to take him back to Siberia. No doubt some Gulag would be his next stop. On their way, Denys and the guards came to a field of corn behind a 4ft stone wall. Denys sized up the two soldiers and decided they would not pursue him if he bolted.

He dashed to the wall and cleared it with ease. The soldiers fired a couple of shots but missed as he ran through the tall corn and returned to the base, where the authorities issued papers registering him as a Polish citizen. Most of the men over twenty were born in the Austrian Empire. Poland was an independent country for only 19 years.

Denys embarked on a ship for Pahlavi, but a Pole from his locality in Ukraine recognized him and informed other Poles Denys was Ukrainian. They grabbed him and tossed him overboard. They now had the upper hand and took revenge on the hateful Ukrainians. He would have died, but a passing fishing boat crew saw what happened and picked him up.

The women and children followed the trek to Krasnovodsk. They stopped at the Aral Sea, where some drowned trying to clean themselves of the lice. The wives whose husbands moved on to the Middle East had permission to board a vessel bound for Persia.

When Olena came to the registration station to continue her journey, she said her husband was Denys. The registrar told her that his wife Aniela already boarded the ship and that Olena was an imposter.

Devastated at being betrayed by a woman she saved from starvation, Olena and her children were shipped back to the internment camp in Siberia. Olena fell sick from Typhoid and perished with her daughter, leaving Vasyl an orphan.

The child would have died, but Alyosha Gunaev, who drove the cart collecting bodies, noticed that the toddler lying beside his dead mother was still breathing. At first, he thought he would leave him to die, but after talking with his wife, the couple agreed to keep the child.

Alyosha did not know the name or nationality of the boy. He had two distinguishing marks split left earlobe and a burn mark on his forearm. The Russian decided to name him after his father, Onufry Gunaev.

CHAPTER 6

Alyosha Gunaev kept the baby he named Onufry for a year until his wife became ill and passed away.

Not knowing how to cope with the child, he gave the toddler to an orphanage run by a relative, a woman who was a nun hiding from the communist authorities.

The communists hunted down the faithful and exterminated the bishops and priests between 1919 and 1923. By 1936, only a few clergy remained hiding underground in obscure places like Camp Sorcery.

Stalin was a former seminarian who understood the effect of faith on people's minds. Though he despised religion as the opiate of the masses, with the rout of the Soviet Forces by Hitler in 1942, Stalin could not afford to have a disunited nation.

In a sinister move, he decided to resurrect the Orthodox Church and turn it into an agency that would bring out the faithful from hiding and, at the same time, serve as an informant to the KGB as part of the Kremlin's control over the people.

Butin

To the outside world, the act made the communist regime appear tolerant of religion.

Stalin gathered what remained of the Christian community in the USSR and some of those who fled abroad, like Gunaev's relatives, and used them as guides to train his informants, dress them in proper attire, and teach them the behavior expected from a real Church.

Thus, Stalin created the new Russian Orthodox Church, pretending it was a rehabilitation of the exterminated czarist Church.

With Stalin's 1942 religious initiative, Onufry's nanny became a rehabilitated nun. She took Onufry to an orphanage where she could keep an eye on him and where he grew up until the priest who administered sacraments at the nunnery asked him to be an acolyte.

It turned out that Kaska was shipped to Russia and wound up working in the convent as an assistant to Mother Superior. She recognized her sister's son Vasyl by his birthmarks and told Onufry she was his aunt.

Onufry did not know what to believe and asked her not to tell anyone because he did not remember her. Kaska was a total stranger, and he knew Alyosha was his father. However, she became protective of him as a sort of atonement for what she did to her sister, who perished in Siberia.

Jason Wright

The saintly acolytes were obedient and eager to serve God, but the priest had more than heavenly service on his mind. He abused the boy. Kaska discovered what was happening and informed Mother Superior, who banned the visiting priests from the convent.

As an orphan with no relatives and having spent his life with nuns as an aid to priests, there were no objections to him becoming a priest. Onufry became one at thirty.

Aware of the sexual abuse by the clergy and the fact priests served as secret police informants, he gained total disdain for the formalities of religion. His belief in God as the creator of the Universe was fundamental, but he did not subscribe to the church's dogma.

That did not mean he would not take advantage of the system to gain a better life. He thought a person did not need a church or a priest to intercede with the Lord on his behalf. In his opinion, the church should serve as a social place for community gatherings and commemorations of religious holidays. However, he stayed quiet about his thoughts that the Church elders would consider heresy.

Most priests married and raised families. Those who did not marry had liaisons with women secretly because marriage precluded them from moving higher up in the Church administration.

Butin

Onufry was not a homosexual, but he was not drawn to matrimony because his childhood experience traumatized him to sexual relationships.

He was content with leading an exemplary life while serving the fishing village of Ust Luga and other nearby settlements. The service provided him with the respect accorded to a holy person.

The hierarchy noticed his exceptional conduct, and the Patriarch of Moscow consecrated him as a bishop of the area to replace the old one who passed away from lung cancer.

Onufry was tolerant of other religions, although the Stalinist Church vigorously persecuted other Christian faiths. He did not despise the Jews. He respected their ancient custom and religion but resented their pursuit of money whenever they infringed on the Church's affairs.

While many priests acted as informants and reported to the authorities any activity which they thought seditious, Onufry refused to betray his faithful, keeping their confessions sacred.

They were simple folks harmless to the state and rarely disobeyed the Kremlin's edicts. Besides, everybody in Russia spied on their neighbor to gain favor with the police or to betray them out of jealousy.

Onufry made one secret unforgivable mistake. During his priesthood, he met the GRU assassin Efrem, whose son was abused by the same man who molested him while he was an altar boy. The assassin asked for access to the nearby monastery to kill the rogue priest.

Onufry's aid to the murder was indefensible, an act that could preclude him from becoming a bishop. From then on, he had to cooperate with the agency to provide clerical cover for assassins.

Years later, Efrem came to see him again at the Nevsky Monastery. He needed a disguise as a bishop for his mission in the US.

CHAPTER 7

Oleg Butin was a tightly built man slightly above five feet tall with light brown hair and blue eyes. His short stature made him self-conscious and prompted him to become competitive and belligerent. He was assigned to recruit spies to further the advancement of the communist microchip industry centered in Dresden, but these were the changing times of the late 1980s.

The drive for the reunification of Germany was in full swing. Gribov, the leader of Russia, highly unpopular with the communist hierarchy, was trying to improve Russia's relationship with the US by relaxing the emigration of the Jews.

He declared himself the president of the Soviet Union and decided the country should ditch the Marxist system and move toward social democracy. Oleg knew the USSR would undergo an upheaval but could do little about it. He was just a junior KGB operative.

Butin met his friend who worked at VEB, an East German manufacturer of electronic components and computer assembly outfit. Sitting in a bar in East Berlin, they exchanged a few pleasantries and case prospects.

"Hans, I have a prospect for you. A closet homosexual working in Fairchild industries in the US visited Frankfurt during a conference last month. Gretchen has him on a film cassette in a sexual act with a teenage boy. She is coming here to give it to you so you can pass it on to Dietrich.

"Sometimes I feel I'm just a messenger. I don't know how long they will keep me in Dresden. There are rumors that Gribov will be removed from power and the KGB chief, Alexander Butin, will become the next leader. Also, the mayor of Moscow wants to take over the leadership and democratize Russia."

"Oleg, that is ridiculous. Russia has never been anything other than a totalitarian country with an absolute dictator in charge of everything. Russians pretend to be Christian, but their real god is the strong man in Kremlin. Your people have the mentality of Genghis Khan.

"The collectivist economy is a failure. Russia needs a leader guided by a Western economist who understands how free trade and private ownership works."

"You sound like a fucking Vlasovite. Vlasov advocated that we should have a czar advised by Germany's chancellor," replied Oleg.

"Why not? For centuries, Russia was governed by German czars, and backward as it was in those days, it could at least feed itself. The communists decided to follow Marxist ideology. They do not understand that Marx proposed his plan for an advanced society, not a primitive one like Russia, where his ideas would not work.

"I'm telling you, Germany will be reunited, and the Warsaw Pact will disappear as if it never existed."

"How can you be so certain? Our troops are still in charge here and in all other vassal states. The demise of our military arrangement would imply the disappearance of the Kremlin's influence outside of Russia."

"Countries like Poland and Czechoslovakia never wanted to be associated with Russia because they have always been pro-Western. It's not just because they are Catholic. The Baltic republics and Ukraine consider themselves European rather than Russian," replied Hans.

"You may be right about the Balts, but the suggestion Ukraine would leave the USSR is ridiculous. They are Russian people."

"That's what you and most of you Russians think and have been told to believe, but you are wrong. You have never lived in Ukraine, so you do not know them. Ukrainians and Russians are very different nations who speak similar languages corrupted by three hundred years of Russian colonialism, just as English influenced the Irish."

"Without Ukraine, we would cease to be an empire. To Russians, losing Ukraine is unthinkable."

"Oleg, you have been brainwashed by the outdated ideas of people like Kissinger and Brzezinski. Russia would become an Asian country if it lost Ukraine unless it rid itself of the Central Asian Republics, but it still would be a huge and powerful state.

"Mark my word, the USSR will disintegrate, and all your espionage efforts here will amount to nothing, so you may as well relax and shag your partner as usual."

"I can't stop seeing her because she's the go-between me and our asset in England. My spouse bitches about her, but I have known her for a long time. I keep telling my wife it is nothing serious because we are just having fun."

Gretchen came to the pub.

"Hans and Oleg, what are you two up to? I just came from the main office. They are shredding all the documents at the Stasi headquarters because the Berlin Wall is coming down. All hell is breaking loose. Everybody quit their jobs and hid, scared they may be accused of murder and brutality after the reunification.

"I brought you the cassette, Hans. You can deliver it to Dietrich. The man in the tape is working on a new GaAs chip. It is a first-order transition material a hundred times faster than silicon structures, and they can mount it on silicon substrates even though the lattice sizes do not match.

"He is an easy mark, and he will cooperate with us because if Fairchild finds out he's a homosexual, he will lose his job and security clearance. Also, he's a family man, so his wife will divorce him if she finds out.

"Speaking of wives, Oleg, is yours still bitching about me?"

"Not so much anymore because I explained to her, we were just friends and told her you are married."

"Does that mean you can spend the night and give me some loving care?

"There is a bottle of schnapps and a fifth of vodka at my place if you want to act like macho Russian. I don't drink straight alcohol. I stock it for you."

"The two of you don't need a third wheel around, so I'll move along. I came because Oleg told me you had important evidence, so if you let me have it, I will give it to my boss."

Hans said his goodbyes and departed after Gretchen gave him the cassette.

"My car is parked in the grocery lot. Why don't I drive because I hate that Soviet junk you call a car. Before we leave, I'll stop at the store and get some cheese and sausage."

"Gretchen, I can't stay the night. As it is, Masha will have a fit about this."

"Fine, I can drop you off here afterward."

She drove to her apartment building and took Oleg up to her suite. They entered the living room with an open kitchen and a dining area. A sliding door opened to a balcony.

"Make yourself comfortable. Fix a plate of sausage and cheese while I change. You can find the cinnamon schnapps and vodka in the cabinet above the counter."

The place was neat. Besides the living room-kitchen combination, a door led to a bedroom with a queen-sized bed, an oak headboard, and two side tables. A side window looked out on the street and high-rise buildings.

On the other side of the room was the bathroom.

He took out a couple of glasses, cut up the sausage and the cheese, and arranged them neatly on a platter on the dining room table.

Gretchen came out wearing a see-through negligee. She was a busty blonde four inches taller than Oleg.

"Come here, little Russian."

She walked up, took his head, and squeezed his face between her breasts.

Let us sit down, and I'll teach you how to play Checkers. I'll let you have your way with me if you win."

"Who the heck are you kidding, woman? You always wind up on top of me, even when I beat you."

Gretchen laughed while pouring the drinks.

"What are you going to do if Russia leaves East Germany?"

"I have no idea. We phoned Moscow asking for help and instructions and received no reply. The Kremlin treats us as if we did not exist. It appears Gribov wants the West to take over East Germany. The headquarters will reassign me to someplace in Russia. My job here would make little sense if we abandoned East Germany."

"Why don't you defect to the West and live in Germany?"

"As a KGB, what would I do in the West?"

"I will miss you."

They played two games, and Gretchen won both times.

"Oleg, you want to be on top?"

"No, have your way as usual."

"Why don't you try straddling me and come between my tits when you get your second wind? You always liked my boobs."

Oleg came home at two am. His wife was furious.

"The least you could do is shower afterward. I hate the smell of that bitch on you."

"She is not a whore. How often must I tell you it's part of my job? We work together, and we often act as if we were a couple. She's my friend. There is no love involved."

"Like hell, there isn't. You snuck around behind my back before you took up with Gretchen."

CHAPTER 8

The Soviet Union dissolved in 1991, and the chief of the KGB, Sasha Butin, was replaced by his second in command, Perion Volkoff, who gathered the head of the GRU, bosses of the crime families, heads of the government, and the patriarch of the Orthodox Church to a meeting.

First, he informed them he was the boss of the FSB, the renamed KGB, and intended to run the show according to his rules. Then he said that the new Russia became the Russian Federation and would operate using a pseudo-democratic system.

The meaningless paper laws that existed under communist rule would now become real. The courts would abide by the laws and render decisions without input from the President, except in cases involving espionage and foreign policy.

The Mafia would no longer be associated with or answer to the Kremlin. Instead, it would be subject to the written Laws. The Church would act as a Christian entity, although it would still perform its role as the informant to the FSB.

With the collapse of the USSR and the loss of prisoner nations and vassal states of Eastern Europe, the official KGB operations outside of Russia were closed down.

Oleg Butin was assigned as an assistant to the Mayor of St. Petersburg, a forward-looking man who wanted to administer the city as a democracy. Oleg acted as the security man dealing with the Mafia owned by Oleg's grade school classmate.

He met his childhood buddy Igor, the boss of a criminal family, in a local bar to tell him to make peace between gangs and stop the frequent killings that made the city look bad to outsiders.

"So, the head office of the secret police transferred you here. What are you doing?"

"Not much. Except I resigned from the KGB to become a civil servant. According to my job description, I am supposed to be the liaison who brings investments to St. Petersburg, but I serve more as a bodyguard," replied Oleg

"You are in luck because I know the oil baron Felstein, who owns the major oil company in town. With your connection with the secret police and the government, we can make a mint, and I can leave the dope and prostitution racket to my cousin Vadim. We can make millions of dollars in politics.

"The Oligarch would like to build an oil exporting terminal in Ust Luga on the church property of bishop Onufry, who will not allow the development unless he gets 50% ownership of the proposed business."

"Igor, Ust Luga is a river delta, mostly swamp. It is close to the Estonian border and not within our city's jurisdiction. What makes you think I can help you?" Said Oleg as he sat back to hear what his buddy had on his mind.

"You know the FSB chief Volkoff, why don't you ask him to tell his eminence to back off?"

Igor explained that President Maximov was pushing for building an Industrial port at the mouth of the Luga River. He gave up on the idea because he became preoccupied with the conflict in Chechnya and the denuclearization of independent Ukraine.

Igor said if Oleg managed to bring the shipping port into being, he would gain access to Maximov as the prime mover of his pet industrialization project. It would be his ticket to promotion as a high government official.

He also pointed out that money is the key to progress. Oleg could use a financial sponsor like Felstein. Russia is changing, and he would never have a better chance to move forward. Oligarchs have money and own most of the wealth in the country.

Onufry is unreasonable in his demand from Jew Felstein. If Oleg could help Felstein acquire the property of the Orthodox Patriarchy, the oligarch would finance his advancement in the administration.

"You know that bribes are essential for upward mobility in civil service. Why would you want to be stuck acting as Mayor Peskov's bodyguard?" Concluded Igor.

"I'll do as you suggest. If I ask Volkoff to resolve the impasse, the worst he can do is to turn me away. If I can present the construction of the oil terminal as a badly needed project for the development of our economy, he might help us. The pompous ass fancies himself as white night, the savior of Russia."

"Why don't you have Peskov arrange a meeting between you, Felstein, and Lypinsky? Both tycoons are eager to develop Ust Luga. With two developers involved in the project, you can play them off against each other to gain their trust, and there will be less corruption with two players rather than one. If they sponsor you financially, you can climb the administrative ladder until you replace Volkoff."

"I'm not interested in replacing him and becoming the leader of the FSB. As I told you, I want to work in the government. FSB's career is a dead end. I had my fill of espionage in Germany, where I was a messenger boy between the Stasi and the KGB," replied Oleg

"I know you, Igor. You are not bringing up this deal on the spur of the moment. You schemed about it for a long time. So, tell me, what do you expect to get out of this?"

"I'll be your silent partner because I have a criminal record. I want the federal police to leave me alone instead of sticking their nose in my business. The cops want to muscle in on my drug deals. How about you promise to give me a five percent stake in the oil terminal, and if you succeed, I'll let you have a third of our take from the dope smuggling?

"You can tell the two oligarchs you will be the facilitator between them and the Church because you know the FSB Chief.

"Volkoff considers politicians, the Mafia, and Jewish oligarchs as lowlifes, so he will not ask you for a bribe because he fancies himself as incorruptible," concluded Igor sarcastically.

"You have a deal, Igor, if you promise to stay out of sight and clamp down on Mafia killings. Peskov has been after me to clean up the town because he wants the city to be respectable enough to draw in business from the US. Otherwise, he will keep bugging me about the Mafia instead of working on our proposal with the two oligarchs."

They were ready to leave when Oleg's old flame Irina came in to join them and ordered a Screw Driver.

"Hi gorgeous, remember Oleg?"

"How is life treating you, ladybug?"

"Nobody has called me that since you left for Dresden. I got divorced last year from Petr. I was tired of army life. I did not want to go to Chechnya with him.

"My daughter Natasha joined the GRU. She wants to live abroad and is enamored with the US entertainers and American music.

"My youngest, Anna, is in London. She married a horny Englishman who works for AB Airlines. So, now I live alone. Other than that, not much else changed. Yesterday, I got a job as a receptionist at PTK company.

"You have not changed much outside of thinning hair. When did you get back from Germany? How come you haven't called?"

"I got back in 1992 to work for the City's Foreign Relations office, but in reality, I'm the Mayor's bodyguard and in charge of bringing industrial investment to St. Petersburg. My family life is the same, except my wife isn't bitching as much about my screwing around as she did about my affair with my contact Gretchen."

"No need to change now. You can come by my place like in the good old times before I married Petr."

The trio parted. Igor left first after arranging to meet Oleg once he met with Volkoff. Irina invited Oleg to her house for the weekend.

CHAPTER 9

Oleg asked Mayor Peskov to convene a meeting with him, Felstein, and Lypinsky. He proposed to serve as their facilitator for the industrial development of Ust Luga in Bishop Onufry's parish.

The boss asked what he and his city would gain by getting involved in the venture. Oleg said all the business offices and trade transactions would go through St. Petersburg, and the booster pumping station for natural gas would be built within city limits on his property.

The Oligarchs came to the city hall two days later. Oleg suggested meeting on their behalf with the FSB Volkoff, the only person able to persuade his eminence Onufry to allow the relocation of a church and the village to clear the Luga delta for sale to the shipping enterprises.

The police Chief refused to meet the investors directly. He detested them as corrupt individuals responsible for bringing down the communist system.

The project required uprooting the homes and the traditional occupation of the faithful. Most likely, the usual activity of the local people would be terminated.

The original Izhorian people of the area vanished. Stalin deported them to Siberia, where they perished from hunger.

The Russian population that replaced them had a fishing dock that would need to be removed. The occupation of the villagers as fishermen would end, but they would have the opportunity to work for better pay at the new businesses.

The proposed deal stipulated that Felstein's crude oil and natural gas outlets would share the coastal property with Lypinsky's terminal for coal and fertilized export. The two developers would locate their businesses on opposite banks of the river. The administrative offices of the outfits would be housed in the city.

Oleg suggested to the buyers he and his silent partner would each receive three percent ownership of both businesses. The six percent cut sounded much better than the unreasonable fifty percent interest demanded by Onufry because he was against the project.

When the oligarchs questioned Oleg about his associate, he did not mention Igor, only said that his colleague would protect their businesses since every business in Russia needed protection from racketeers.

When they asked Oleg if he could deliver on his proposal, he told them if he did not, they would lose nothing. He wasn't sure if Volkoff would help, but he met the KGB chief several times at the headquarters in Germany.

Peskov volunteered to arrange an exploratory session between Volkoff and Oleg, the latter representing the two tycoons. If the Commandant consented to the proposed venture, he would be asked to invite the bishop to meet Oleg and work out a deal for the land.

In response to the mayor's request, Volkoff agreed to see Oleg because the president wanted to build a deep-sea port at the mouth of the Luga River to avoid dealing with the Estonian Customs. During the USSR, Russia's shipping went through the adjacent Estonia, now an independent state.

The chief remembered Oleg, a former KGB officer, from his tour of Germany. However, he knew him from a time before they met in Dresden.

Volkoff summoned Butin for a meeting at the secret police headquarters in Moscow. Oleg had the authority to offer Volkoff and the Bishop ten million dollars each to acquire the property. He felt the amount would be insufficient because Onufry could extract much more from both oligarchs.

Oleg doubted that his pretentious host would ask for a bribe because he considered himself incorruptible. He waited two hours to see Volkoff. When the chief came, dressed meticulously as usual, he towered over Oleg, intimidating him, and assumed a benevolent, condescending attitude.

How are you, Citizen Gruber? He said as if it was still the USSR.

Oleg hesitated upon hearing his original family name. He did not remember Volkoff as the man who saved him from hanging. He had little memory of the traumatic time when his father died because he remembered only the hangman Fanerik and the screams of his mother, not the commanding officer.

"I apologize for being late. I have no time to spend with you right now. I just came from seeing the president. He told me the war in Chechnya is not going well, and Kuchma is reluctant to give up Ukrainian nukes unless he secures a guarantee for the territorial integrity of Ukraine.

"I have to attend another meeting. I mentioned to him your proposal for the commercial use of the delta. He urged me to convince Onufry to permit the Jews to build their terminals.

"Let's meet with the bishop at noon next Tuesday and work out an acceptable agreement with him. I don't want to strong-arm him. These are modern times of democracy. The Church officials became independent since the fall of the USSR. Now, we ask them to do what we want instead of telling them what to do."

The following week, Oleg and the Chief met with Onufry at the Police headquarters. They sat at a table over a bottle of vodka, bites of black bread, and pickled herring to iron out the deal.

Volkoff introduced Oleg as the assistant to Mayor Peskov and a spokesman for the Jewish oligarchs. He mentioned that the president was enthusiastic about their proposal to build the new shipping terminal.

At first, the bishop was not receptive to the idea but agreed to it when Oleg doubled the bribe to include the money meant for the FSB. He presented the cash as money earmarked for rebuilding the Luga Church further up the river, knowing that a good portion of the funds would wind up in the bishop's coffer.

"The Jews will turn our sacred Christian ground into their capitalist venture. What is the country coming to?" asked Onufry.

Volkoff did not answer but sweetened the deal by promising the Nevsky monastery would become Onufry's new residence, where he would administer the novices preparing to take their first vows.

The bishop would retain his jurisdiction over the Ust Luga parish and train the GRU agents as the representatives of the Russian Orthodox Church to ecumenical councils abroad.

The Chief snuck the GRU training into the agreement as his reward from the deal.

The transaction obliged Felstein to invest three billion dollars in building gas and oil export terminals and a compressor station in St. Petersburg. Lypinsky would dredge a channel for deep sea vessels and build a Fertilizer shipping facility costing half as much.

With the conclusion of the agreement, Oleg climbed the civil service ladder. His negotiating skills gained the president's attention. As Igor predicted, Butin progressed in the Kremlin's hierarchy.

CHAPTER 10

In 1997, the Russian economy was in a downward spiral and collapsed the subsequent year. The ruble was devalued, and the government had difficulty paying its debts. The succession of the events propelled Oleg Butin's career.

He met with FSB chief Volkoff to discuss the economic crisis.

"How are you, Gruber? You made a great stride since the Luga Seaport deal. President Maximov is pleased with your accomplishment in making the deep-sea port a reality."

"How did you know my real name?"

"Don't you remember, I saved you from hanging and sent you to my Chief's cousin in Leningrad?"

"So, you killed my father. Am I supposed to be thankful?"

"Kola Fanerik hung your Vlasov collaborator father. He deserved to die, like all traitors to the motherland. I only spared you from the hangmen.

"Anyway, I summoned you only because the president wants you to work in his administration. He seems to think you understand the Western economy. What do you think we should do to help the economic recovery?"

"I did not pretend to know about the economy, but I have learned how oligarchs bought their ill-gotten gains by cheating the Russian public out of their vouchers with money they got from New York banks. They are the problem our country suffers today.

"The economy cannot be saved with the present pseudo-democratic government in power. The bunglers try to imitate the market economy of the West but have no clue what they are doing. Russia has never been anything but a totalitarian state that people understand and fear. To improve the trade, we need to change the administration."

"I could charge you with treason for such a suggestion, but Maximov wants to appoint you as the deputy chief of staff."

We'll see who charges whom, you pompous bastard, thought Oleg.

Butin met Maximov in his office. He did not know what to expect since there was no invite from the president.

"I'm here because Chief Volkoff sent me to see you about my work on the Ust Luga Deep Seaport."

"I asked Perion to send you. I am impressed with your negotiating skills. How would you like to be my Chief of Staff?"

"I'm flattered, but I'm not an economist, and I cannot change the state of the economy under the present system. If you think I can help, I'll take the job if you give me a free hand rearranging the current administration."

Maximov agreed because he had little choice. After all, Russia was bankrupt. Oleg accepted the appointment as the Chief of Staff and eliminated his potential rivals within the first year.

In 1998, Oleg told Igor's nephew Vadim to assassinate Chief Volkoff, who knew too much about Oleg's origin he wanted to keep secret. To replace him, Maximov appointed Butin to head the FSB.

Having secured control of the FSB, he was ready for the next step to take over the government. He persuaded Maximov to appoint him as the prime minister.

The economy went bankrupt in August 1999 and could not service its foreign debt without defaulting on the loans. Oleg took advantage of the crisis to seize power as Russia's supreme leader.

He confronted Maximov with the new FSB Chief and advised the president to resign and install him as the successor to lead the Russian Federation.

He subsequently assassinated the Mayor of St. Petersburg, a proponent of democracy, and sidelined any viable opposition to a staged election in 2000.

The vote count was superficial. The result was plucked out of the air but designed to sound plausible as if the contest was against genuine opponents.

Everybody on the ballot knew nobody would bother counting the votes, and there was no mechanism to ensure the numbers were real rather than presented as reasonable without arousing any suspicion.

His next step was to remove his former backers from revealing how he came to power. Oleg imprisoned Felstein, and Lypinsky escaped to Egland, where the baron conveniently hung himself in an apparent suicide.

The remaining oligarchs either fled abroad or decided to obey Oleg, stay away from politics, and get out of the way of businesses conducted by Oleg's cronies, relatives, and schoolmates. He formed his loyal inner circle to share the wealth of Russia.

It was understood that oligarchs owned what they said only if Oleg agreed that they did. In many cases, owners were told by the FSB to sign over their enterprises to Igor's mafia.

Oleg made up his previously vague beginnings by officially stating he was born in Leningrad in 1952 as the son of Igor Butin. The couple was still alive and happy to go along with the arrangement. Only a woman from Georgia would not stop saying Oleg was her legitimate son, but the news media were told to ignore her as a nut case but did not kill her.

In 2004, Oleg staged an "election" with no opposition. Again, nobody counted the collected votes. A convenient plausible number for 72% landslide was chosen as the margin of victory. Oleg would not allow his press to claim 99% rout as the heavy-handed communists always claimed, and no one believed. Oleg was an old hand at deception.

With the communist collectivist system discarded, Russia transformed into a genuine Nazified state run by an absolute dictator with a Krupp-style oligarchical economy.

The once-vilified Nazi mentality became Russia's new ideology. After all, Communism and fascism differed only in economic control, not the repressive rule over the masses. The far-right organizations began flourishing in Russia, just as Hitler's brown shirts did in Germany.

CHAPTER 11

Having come to power seemingly out of nowhere, Oleg Butin vowed to resurrect his version of his beloved USSR. His upcoming invasions would challenge the world order established in 1991 after the collapse of the Soviet Empire.

His planned conquests would follow Hitler's example, but he did not want to make them appear as unprovoked assaults like those of Nazis that would alarm NATO. He would disguise them using false flag attacks and fictitious outside provocations.

Butin wanted to present the image of Russia abroad as something other than a totalitarian regime. He wished to portray Russia as a democracy.

Thus, he conducted sham elections to give Russia the appearance of a democratic state. However, the Russian constitution had term limits set during Maximov's reign. Butin would have to relinquish the presidency after he served the second time, something he would not do.

To circumvent the rule, he staged an election in 2008 where his stand-in, Medved, posed as the elected president while Butin held the reins of power as the premier. The shill deferred all decisions to Oleg until he could again run to regain the title.

His first task was to make sure Belarus became the Kremlin's puppet, returning the country to a colonial state administered by a subservient dictator.

He installed a lackey warlord in the rebellious Chechnya after Russia slaughtered a third of its population by bombing Grozny worse than Dresden in WWII.

2008 was a golden opportunity for Russia's territorial expansion because America was distracted by financial turmoil and was unlikely to intervene in Butin's conquests.

The giant US banks, presumably too large to fail, went bankrupt, precipitating the housing crash and bankruptcy of countries like Iceland that invested in bundled Wall Street mortgages.

Since the US was in an economic downturn, the US election in November 2008 was likely to put a Democrat, Hassan, an African-American, in the White House.

Butin reasoned that the lame-duck Republican president would not oppose that year's Russian aggression in the northern part of Georgia, where Moscow planted its men to stage a false flag assault on South Ossetia.

In response to the sham provocation, Russia invaded Georgia. Oleg used the intrusion to test Hassan's reaction to future Russian attacks on its neighbors.

Butin

The Democrat's weak objection to the Russian invasion of Georgia convinced Butin that NATO would not protect the self-determination of Ukraine.

He concluded that the Black man in the White House came from a socialist background supportive of communism and Russia's aspiration to resurrect the USSR.

True to form, the US government did nothing substantial to oppose Butin's de facto annexation of Georgia's two regions, Abkhazia and South Ossetia. Butin decided that the indecisive Hassan would do nothing about his further conquests because he was inexperienced in foreign policy, a weak person Oleg could intimidate with nuclear threats.

His next quest was the territorial conquest of Ukraine. He considered his annexation of Abkhazia to be like Hitler's annexation of Sudetenland, and his occupation of Ukraine would be like the German takeover of Czechoslovakia.

Once Ukraine fell as expected, he would turn his attention to Kazakhstan, where a substantial minority of Russians would be sympathetic to an annexation of that country's mineral-rich Northern region.

Oleg's partner Igor argued that the invasion of Asian Kazakhstan should precede the assault on the brotherly Slavic Ukraine. However, Igor's cousin Vadim persuaded Butin that Ukraine was an easy mark and would not concern China like Kazakhstan would.

Ukraine had no viable army because it relied on the Budapest agreement signed by the US, the UK, and Russia that assured Ukraine's territorial integrity for relinquishing its share of Soviet nukes that were made, outfitted, and stationed in Ukraine.

While the aggression against Georgia used a staged attack as an excuse for the Kremlin's land grab, the same technique would not work in Ukraine.

Eastern Ukrainians, labeled as Russian Speakers, dominated the country's politics. Nobody would believe they attacked Moscow for any reason, let alone to gain territory.

Rather than embarking on a naked strike against Ukraine, Oleg decided to disguise his takeover of Crimea by using what he portrayed as a private Mercenary Army belonging to the narcotics Warlord Igor.

The activities of the mercenaries in the Middle East, Africa, and Ukraine would appear separate from Russia's official business.

The militia consisted of retired Russian soldiers, mafia henchmen, felons, and volunteers drawn into the organization by billing it as a Nazi-style troops of the Wehrmacht bearing the German name Wolfgang.

Igor disguised Butin's intrusions in the civil strife in Syria and Libya and his offensive against unsuspecting Ukraine in

2014 as an act of a Warlord without the Kremlin's participation.

At the time, Ukraine had as its president Moscow's puppet, Yansin, elected by a slim majority, promising he would sign Ukraine's Association Agreement with the EU most Ukrainians wanted.

The traitor stalled on the signing for four years. Instead, he took a bribe from the Kremlin of two billion dollars to renege on his election promise. The betrayal outraged the voters. Some two hundred thousand people from all regions of Ukraine protested for six months against the president's welching on the signature.

The protest presented Butin with an opportunity to invade Crimea and Eastern Ukraine by pretending it was a response to America's ambassador orchestrating the dissent. The mercenaries wearing Russian army uniforms stripped of insignia poured into Crimea through the Naval base Russia leased from Ukraine in Sevastopol.

Ukrainian Military had no guidance or orders from the treacherous Yansin to resist the invaders. Its soldiers were told to remain in their barracks while the disguised militia took over the peninsula. Crimea fell with only a few casualties and one official killing reported.

As Oleg expected, President Hassan condemned the invasion but did nothing to honor the pledge to preserve the territorial integrity of Ukraine, promised when Ukraine gave up its nukes. The other signatories of the agreement followed the US lead in appeasing Butin, who issued a veiled threat of World War if they interfered.

To subdue dissent in Ukraine, he thought he could quell the uprising by sending in shooters to assassinate the prominent leaders of the movement in Kyiv. The snipers killed a hundred protesters, causing the dissent to turn violent. Fearing for his life, Yansin fled to Russia with his bribe after the people assaulted the killers to stop the assassinations.

Yansin's flight to Moscow precipitated the Kremlin's intrusion into Donbas under the leadership of Transnistria's Colonel Gorkov, leading the mercenaries the West called the "little green men" whom the Kremlin billed as "Ukrainian Rebels" even though it was entirely Russian.

The disguised invaders, supported by the Russian army, outnumbered and outmatched the Ukrainian defenders, turning the conquest into a frozen struggle between the Ukrainians and Igors's hirelings.

During the conflict, the occupiers shot down the Dutch passenger plane MH17, killing all aboard, and blamed Kyiv's forces for the crime.

The appeasement of Butin, by the abandonment of Ukraine, propelled him to further military adventures.

Butin

Following Hitler's example of intruding into the civil war in Spain, Butin intruded into conflicts in Syria and Africa by using his proxy Wolfgang, whom Igor transformed into a potent terrorist force.

Hassan again made superficial objections to the intrusions that Butin shrugged off.

Butin's subsequent move was to ensure the 2016 American election chose a president as favorable to Russian territorial expansion as Hassan was.

To achieve this, he groomed Doug Trimm, a former Tea Party member who adored him. The radical Party was a dead end, but when Trimm switched from the Democratic Party to the Republican Party, he became Oleg's choice as the leader of the GOP. The political faction in the US sympathetic to Butin infiltrated the Republicans under the slogan "Make America Great Again."

Trimm was Russia's ideal candidate who would serve the Kremlin by dismantling NATO and allowing Oleg to reclaim the territories Russia lost with the dissolution of the USSR.

To elect Trimm, Butin needed to influence the electorate to support him. His KGB experience from the days of the Cold War came in handy. Soviet Union had cadres of propagandists who could train bloggers in propaganda factories to inundate the worldwide Net with lies directed to persuade US blue-collar workers to vote for Trimm.

Moscow would also buy the services of popular TV influencers, such as Truson, who dominated the American conservative media. The newscasters would brainwash their followers to follow Trimm. In particular, Butin's efforts would concentrate on one-issue voters, the Evangelical anti-abortion movement, and the NRA gun rights enthusiasts.

CHAPTER 12

The road to Nevsky Monastery was a narrow cobblestone pathway barely wide enough for his car. Both sides of the driveway were wooded, so he could not turn back unless he drove to the gate.

At the guard house, an armed FSB approached him.

"What is your business here?"

"I am Efrem. I have an appointment with Patriarch Onufry. He is expecting me."

The officer phoned to confirm the meeting and told him to drive his vehicle off to the side and leave it there before he came into the compound.

When he worked his way to the monastery, a monk greeted him at the door and took him to the waiting room.

"Please make himself comfortable until I return."

Half an hour later, the novice came back to take him to see his host.

His eminence sat at a table in plain clothes and a drink. Efrem expected him to be dressed in the usual Russian Orthodox garments.

"What is your poison?" He asked in English.

"How about a couple of fingers of a single malt scotch I just got from the US?"

Before his puzzled guest could answer, he poured him a four-finger shot into a narrow glass.

"I understand the GRU headquarters assigned you to be our representative in the Ecumenical Council of Christians."

"Yes, I came to be briefed on my mission and outfitted with proper attire for the job."

"You will undergo ten days of training in the history and the religious manners of the Russian Orthodox Church and another two weeks to familiarize yourself with the background of your host."

"You will be the guest of reverend Fallworth, an influential man in the republican party with connections to the US military."

"Your assignment is urgent because it concerns the presidential elections in the US. We need an American president sympathetic to Russia and our plan to invade Ukraine to restore Russia to the historical legacy of Stalin and Czar Peter the Great."

Onufry leaned back to explain to Efrem the history of the Orthodox Church and how the GRU became part of the Christian mission in America.

Butin

"Butin intends to conquer democratic Ukraine without Americans coming to its aid. Russia must reconquer it to regain its status as a global power.

"Our propaganda over the centuries built the image of Ukraine as an essential component of the Russian Empire. Since we lost Ukraine as our colony, the world has taken us for granted, saying we are just another country with oil and a nuclear arsenal.

"The President wants to restore the imperial Russia. He will use the threat of nuclear war to keep the West from aiding Ukraine and confine the conflict, if there is one, to the territory of Ukraine.

"Ukrainians are oblivious to our intentions. They are unarmed because they believe the guarantees of territorial integrity they received from the nuclear powers, in exchange for giving up their nuclear deterrent in the early 1990s."

"Did not Russia sign the agreement as well as the US and Britain?" interjected Efrem

"Of course, that is how we duped them into believing they are safe without an army," replied Onufry, somewhat irritated by the interruption.

"Your American host Fallworth has the following of the Evangelical Conference. The Evangelicals and the NRA are the two very influential political groups in the USA whom we must convince to nominate Trimm, the candidate of our choice, for the next presidency of the US.

"You will cooperate with novice Nadia, a presentable GRU agent whose assignment is to bribe Truson, the persuasive commentator of the leading Conservative news Network, to support our cause. She will persuade him to promote Trimm as the Republican nominee for the upcoming US election.

"Understand that propaganda on the worldwide Net often decides the outcome of conflicts as much as any military operation. Persuading the American masses to our point of view will allow Trimm to aid Butin by undermining America from within.

"The perception people have about world affairs wins elections, not facts and reality," said Onufry as he sat back to educate Efrem about the historical background of the current Orthodoxy in Russia

The Orthodox Church had a prominent place in the czarist Empire. The czar was its head equal in importance to God, and his portrait hung at the altar beside the icon of Jesus.

The communists annihilated Christianity after the revolution. Between 1919 and 1923, all formal religions disappeared with the eradication of clergy and the destruction of the churches.

The persecution of religion in the USSR lasted for another ten years, the decade when the Bolsheviks murdered millions of Christians and drove the believers to hide from the authority. The secret police gained total control of the country when Stalin took over in 1930, except for the Christian underground.

Stalin understood the hold religious faith had on the people even though he despised religion. His understanding came from the fact that, as a young man, he was a seminarian expelled from the monastic order for declaring religion was the opiate of the masses.

The WWII conflict turned against Russia in 1942, and Stalin felt he needed the support of all citizens to unite behind his war effort.

His idea for achieving unity was brilliant.

He accomplished his purpose by bolstering the effectiveness of the KGB with a network of informants the population could trust rather than fear. As a sinister mockery of Christianity, Stalin dressed the informant agents in the robes of the extinct czarist clergy. Thus, he created the present-day Orthodox informant agency of the Russian Federation.

Stalin knew the remnant Christians hiding underground would be deceived by the clerical attire and come out in the open, trusting the new churchmen. Through this act, Stalin accomplished two results. He extended the reach of the police to the Christian community and united the masses in his struggle against the Nazis.

The creation of the Church also resulted in generous American aid to the Soviet war effort that turned the conflict in favor of the Communists in 1943.

The false resurrection of Orthodoxy provides the Kremlin with a mantle of legitimacy and ambiguity. Russia appears more tolerant of religion, shedding its past image of godlessness. The disguise is intentional because we believe familiarity and predictability by outsiders threaten our state.

The successive administrations that followed the reign of Stalin discouraged religion but did not destroy it. However, despite the efforts to govern the vast Empire, the USSR failed to establish a sustainable economy. It could not feed its people until Ukraine instituted a quota exchange program that wrestled the agriculture of Ukraine from central control.

Ukrainians showed the collectivist economy was an abject failure and needed to be abolished. They proved the communist system dysfunctional. When Ukraine quietly declared independence, the USSR and its communist authority collapsed.

With the demise of communism, Maximov, who presided over the dissolution of the Soviet Union, tried to bring Russia back to its historical prominence.

He reinstated the czarist emblems and the original names of the cities and established a pseudo-privatized economy. Maximov pushed the country toward democracy over the objection of the former communist hierarchy that was adamantly against it.

He prevailed over the communists, and as a sign of his determination to democratize the country, he instituted a lower and upper house of parliament. For the first time in history, Russia held two seemingly democratic elections, albeit with no viable opposition or meaningful supervision.

The legislature rubber-stamped his decisions, and the semi-free economy wound up in the hands of super-rich Jewish oligarchs who drained the country of finances, unintentionally precipitating a financial default in 1999 that destroyed the fledgling democracy.

The KGB removed Maximov and installed Butin as the new President, returning the country to the totalitarian system it always had. Russia again became a dictatorship ruled by a strong man, an absolute dictator the people would fear and obey.

Butin got rid of the unruly oligarchs who either fled abroad or whom he murdered and replaced with barons who served him just as Krupp served Hitler.

He still staged meaningless elections to disguise Russia as a democracy. However, in an ironic twist, he emulated Hitler, who dreamed of Russia governed by an authoritarian czar advised by the German chancellor.

Russia now became what it professed to hate, a Nazi-style regime, cloaked as a pretend democracy with czarist trappings, fictitious religion, and an economy run by oligarchs answering to the dictator guided by a former chancellor of Germany.

Butin elevated the Moscow Patriarchy to the stature it had during the time of the czars. The Church regained its prominence, but its mission as an informant network remained the same as in the Stalin era.

He gave the Orthodox Church additional responsibility as the housing authority and the training of the GRU espionage agents to provide them with a perfect cover as the ecumenical clergy.

Efrem became a part of the new organization. He would serve as the bishop, the head of the Russian delegation to the Council of World Churches in the US.

CHAPTER 13

Bishop Efrem and Nadia prepared for a meeting with the influential Charismatic Leader Fallworth to discuss the state of the Baptist congregations of Russia, often referred to as the *Shtundists,* a reference to their one-hour Sunday worship compared with the lengthy Orthodox service.

"We need to ensure the Evangelicals nominate government officials favorable to the Kremlin in the coming 2016 election. We must convince the reverend to endorse Trimm and ask him to persuade his followers to choose him as the Republican nominee," said Efrem.

"According to my orders, persuading the pastor is your assignment, your eminence, and mine is to make sure Mr. Truson persuades his audience on the Net to support the candidate of our choice by disseminating our propaganda on his nightly talk shows and discredit the woman likely to be the Democratic contender."

"Right, I did not mean to imply our tasks are connected. My mission is to persuade Evangelical leaders to endorse Trimm. Their endorsement is crucial because the electorate is evenly split, and the Evangelicals can tip the election in favor of the Republicans."

"You must ensure we have the services of Truson to persuade the blue-collar workers to turn out to vote for the GOP. I suggested the pastor bring him along today to allow you to speak with Truson without arousing suspicion as meeting him elsewhere would."

Throughout the fifty years before the collapse of the USSR, the communists banned all Christian denominations in Russia except the state-controlled Russian Orthodox Church.

Butin changed that policy by allowing other faiths to practice in Russia. The Russian Federation now appears as a nation tolerant of all religions, but the mission of the Moscow Patriarchy as an informant agency remained the same as in 1942.

Baptists in Russia were no longer forbidden to conduct religious services, but Leader Fallworth worried about the dwindling population of the evangelicals in the country.

Nadia, wearing the attire of a monastic order, greeted the guests at the driveway when they arrived in a black Limousine.

Dressed as a nun, she appeared meek, but underneath her slightly revealing cassock, her well-proportioned body, red hair, and sparkling bright blue eyes screamed sex. She was a seasoned thirty-year-old GRU agent expert in martial arts.

She would not participate in the religious discussion and was there to listen, serve wine, and bribe the Conservative newsman Truson, who accompanied Fallworth to the meetings.

"Leader, welcome to our house. I am the assistant to his worship, Bishop Efrem."

"Your comments at the Ecumenical meeting last night moved me. As Christians, we must keep up the struggle to secure justice for the unborn."

"Sister, I agree with what you said. The unborn should have the same rights as all children. Allow me to introduce my companion, newscaster Carl Truson, one of our faithful. He is a commentator on the conservative network Christian News."

"How nice to meet you in person, Mr. Truson. I am aware of your informative broadcasts. I am Novice Nadia from the Sacred Heart order of the Nevsky Monastery."

She shook hands with the influencer and turned to the guest.

"Leader, shall we go inside so you can discuss with his eminence what is on your mind over a glass of wine?"

The four of them sat around the table, and after an opening blessing from the pastor, they began discussing the plight of the dwindling Protestant community in Russia.

"The seminaries do not offer the young parishioners secure careers as pastors, and Churches suffer from diminishing number of faithful. After President

Maximov relaxed visa requirements, many Baptist faithful emigrated to the EU and America."

The leader nodded in agreement and replied.

"To draw believers to our fold, the church must concentrate on the issues that encourage the faithful to follow the evangelical ideals. We are leading the fight against abortion. The preservation of the life of the unborn is paramount.

"Women have become promiscuous because they can terminate the pregnancy up to three months as a contraceptive rather than an economic necessity.

"Our other issue is the homosexuals who want to legalize their marriages, corrupting the sanctity of the holy matrimony that will degrade the Christian society," concluded Fallworth.

"Guide me, pastor, but I see nobody on the horizon in the two major parties other than Douglas Trimm as the candidate who would support the abolishment of Roe v Wade. If elected, he would nominate Supreme Court justices inclined to overturn the abortion law.

"Doug Timm switched parties several times. He was a Democrat but recently became a Republican and announced his intent to run as the GOP candidate for the US presidency. He has a checkered past, but he is an opportunist who will support your drive against abortion if you endorse him," replied Efrem.

"Your eminence is correct and perceptive about American politics. I agree Trimm is our man, and I can make his candidacy viable if I endorse him."

The bishop smiled at the last comment. He had the Evangelist right where he wanted him.

Meanwhile, Nadia was doing her job. She and the newscaster were listening but contributed little to the discussion. As she got up to pour more wine, she brushed slightly against Truson.

After a while, she suggested the Holy Fathers relax in the parlor to consider religious matters while she and the broadcaster visit on the balcony to discuss his latest question-and-answer session with the TV celebrity Doug Trimm.

Carl was delighted with the suggestion as he fantasized about the nun leading him outside.

"Fancy the surprise, I had no idea nuns cared about politics."

"Servants of God are people and vote like everybody else, but I am a novice, not a nun. I have not taken my first wows yet.

"What do you think of the chances Trimm can be elected? He does not have any political experience. I find it odd that entertainers and TV celebrities with no political background are often elected to the Congress."

Carl enjoyed her company. To impress her, he played up his political importance.

"Getting elected is all about name recognition and sponsorship by lobbies who want to pass laws favorable to their interests. Political candidates need endorsement by wealthy people, religious leaders, and news media personalities with large followings like mine.

"With the advent of the worldwide Net, broadcasters like me have persuasive power far beyond what we once had as newspaper commentators. Today, a popular news outlet can flood the Net with misinformation to propel or destroy the candidacy of a political hopeful.

"Our success in promoting a candidate relies on picking a single issue to increase his political appeal. For instance, scapegoating abortion or gay marriage can enhance the popularity of a politician. Goebbels used Jews as scapegoats to create Hitler's following before WWII. In our case, gays and minorities can be labeled as far-left liberals or de facto communists to have the same effect on the public.

"In the final analysis, broadcasting is like any other job. It is all about money. We are paid to persuade people to rally to a cause and produce high ratings for the news agencies we serve," said Truson as he winked after the self-aggrandizing speech.

Nadia came to the point of her reason for taking the influencer aside.

"His worship Efrem informed me Moscow News supports your broadcast. The head of the agency is prepared to increase his support of your show by quadrupling the fee, provided you disseminate our articles supporting candidate Trimm.

"Of course, you have your style and flare for influencing people, and we do not expect you to parrot the comments of the RT News. We only want you to convey the content of our press to your viewers.

"His worship would like me to confirm if this proposal is agreeable to you. Understand I am nothing more than a messenger in this case. We have no formal arrangements with you. It is all done on mutual trust."

"Excellent, you can tell the bishop we have a deal. The pastor drove me here, but I need to leave. Would you care to drive me to my office at Christian News?"

The American men are so predictable. This idiot thinks he can seduce me. Thought Nadia.

"Let me inform the Eminence we are leaving, and you agree to our proposal."

Nadia walked over to the parlor.

"Your eminence, I am taking Mr. Truson to his workplace. He has to prepare for an interview with the metro housing commissioner."

The novice nodded at Efrem, indicating they had a mutual arrangement with the newscaster. The two departed to the garage, where she and Truson piled into a Camry sedan for the trip.

"Nadia, I was curious if the nuns have to give up sex as part of their vows. It must be hard to abstain for the rest of their lives. The carnal desires do not just vanish."

"I cannot say from experience, but a commitment to Jesus is a pledge to a life with rewards in heaven. Devotion to serving God and society is stronger than the wants of the flesh for those who found grace."

Underneath the saintly veneer is a woman who needs to be screwed. I can see where some ugly broads can forgo sex, but she is not one of them, thought the newscaster.

Arriving at the headquarters, Nadia pulled into the driveway and stopped. Truson put his hand inside her thigh.

"Please remove your hand before I break your arm off."

"Oh, come on, you are not fooling anybody with this attire. We are in this arrangement together."

She grabbed his hand and bent it at the wrist as he yelled with pain. Then she turned, got hold of his hair, and jammed his face into her lap.

"This is as close as you will come to my pussy. Understand your work for us, not the other way around, and if you do not live up to our agreement, I will become your nightmare.

Furthermore, you little worm, you do not touch me unless I say where and when."

"Okay, don't be nasty. What was the rub against my shoulder about?"

"That was to tell you I know all about you. You better not mess around with me. Now get out, go home, and fuck your wife. You can pretend it is me."

As he got out, he said he was sorry.

"Think nothing of it. I like you now that we understand each other."

Fucking money-grubbing hypocrites, I hate the bastards no matter the nationality, even though we use them. The creeps would send their mothers to prison for money. They are disguised pretentious philanders and pedophiles, both he and his leader. They fool the dumb and the gullible, nobody else.

Her next meeting was with her handler at the St. George Church.

CHAPTER 14

Nadia drove to St. Nicholas Russian Orthodox parish, where she attended services every Sunday as a cover to give the appearance she was a devout nun and disguise in the confessional her meetings with Father Semyon, the chief priest, who was an FBI informant.

The priest recruited her to inform on Efrem because he considered Stalin's Church an abomination to Christianity. He felt she would cooperate with him after he heard the story of her life as an orphan in the care of a Stalinist priest who abused her.

She thought informing Semyon about Efrem's meeting with Fallworth was not a betrayal of Russia. Their conversations were not State secrets.

Her experience during Butin's invasion of Ukraine in 2014 made her cooperation with Semyon easier.

She believed Slavic countries ought to respect each other and follow the example of the Scandinavians who lived in harmony and prosperity rather than the hostility the Russian Federation exhibited by intruding into its neighbor's business with the so-called sphere of influence, which stood for colonialism nobody wanted.

She told Semyon that Moscow News hired Truson to push propaganda against the Democratic presidential candidate and that Leader Fallworth would endorse Doug Trimm.

She informed him the FBI should be on the lookout for false information because the Kremlin embarked on an effort to hack into the sites of democratic candidates to find material for a smear campaign.

Russian secret police, the FSB, would engage the services of a Danish Whistleblower, Anders, to pass the incriminating information about Democrats to the FBI chief Copson.

The Public considered the Dane as truthful. Thus, he had enough influence with the voters to swing the election for Trimm if the Bureau published the damning information about the democratic challenger.

Nadia could not tell Semyon if Anders worked for the FSB or if Kremin fooled him to serve as their conduit by convincing him he was doing civic duty.

She informed the priest Russia disguised its connection to Truson through a private agreement to hide the fact the Kremlin was involved in the US elections. Moscow News bribed him to air Russian disinformation on his nightly shows supporting Trimm and praising Butin.

As the election grew closer, it was evident the abrasive TV celebrity Trimm would be the nominee of the Republican party, bypassing a well-qualified legislator, a former Midwestern governor.

The Democrats would nominate a woman who served as the Secretary of State in Hassan's administration but never held an elected office. The election became a tight race between the two controversial candidates.

After the nominations were over, the Kremlin's propaganda machine managed to hack the email site of the Democratic candidate and uncovered classified emails on her private server that should not have been there because they were not secure.

The Russians quickly passed what they discovered to the Whistleblower, who turned the emails into the central issue of the election campaign, contending she was irresponsible with government secrets.

Several news polls showed the election was a dead heat, with the Democrats having a tiny lead, until Bûtin's FSB executed a brilliant coup to tip the balance in favor of Trimm. It repackaged her old emails and presented them to Anders as new.

The Dane forwarded the information to Copson, who announced in the media that he found a new email scandal the day before the election.

Nadia informed Semyon about the deception, but he did not have enough time to warn the FBI about the ruse.

Butin

As the result of the misinformation that could not be challenged until after the election, Trimm won by a slim margin. He thanked the chief for publishing it but, true to his vindictive character, trashed him soon afterward.

Moscow celebrated the win with a gala party thrown by Butin in Trimm's honor and Russia's feat in electing its asset as the president of America.

Grooming Trimm as Moscow's asset began decades ago. The FSB studied and entertained him for twenty years before the 2016 election to find weaknesses in his flawed character.

The agency concluded that flattery and sexual liaisons were his weak points. Butin invited him to Russia, where he provided him with lavish accommodations and erotic entertainment, all recorded as potential sources of blackmail. Oleg praised Doug as the most important man of the century.

After he assumed power, Trimm rewarded Butin by trashing the American intel agencies as incompetent and labeled the US military leaders as corrupt businessmen. He also thrashed the rank and file as suckers and losers.

Next, Butin directed Trimm against NATO. The Organization stood in the way of Oleg's desire to carve out of Lithuania a land corridor to Kaliningrad. The Kremlin put out a barrage of propaganda pretending NATO's expansion to the Warsaw Pact countries posed a threat to Russia and asked Trimm to disband it.

Trimm obliged by demanding the EU pay much more for the cost of NATO, hoping the Europeans would object and leave the Alliance because it was too costly.

Trimm's effort to bully the Allies did not produce the desired outcome, but Oleg was undeterred. He had many other tasks in mind for his American admirer.

Following the election, Efrem told Nadia the headquarters recalled her to Moscow. When she asked him if he knew why, he informed her she would serve as the only translator in Butin's private one-on-one meeting with the US president.

Truson recommended her to Trimm as a trustworthy apolitical interpreter, and Butin agreed with the suggestion, knowing she was GRU. The newscaster did it because he thought she would be his exclusive source of what went on at the get-together between the two leaders.

Little did he know, she planned to use their liaisons to remove him from Christian News. Before she departed, she hoped to meet the owner of Network to expose the treacherous broadcaster for undermining America's democracy with his pro-Kremlin agenda.

CHAPTER 15

Nadia was born in Berdsk, a child of parents shipped there as slave labor to maintain the Trans-Siberian railway. Her folks belonged to the Shpot family of Hutsuls from Western Ukraine, deported to Siberia by the Soviet authorities as subversives.

Labeling people as enemies of the state was often used as an excuse to ship Ukrainians to labor camps in the Siberian taiga. The tradition was older than communism. It was also the favorite ploy of the czars to provide the sparsely populated Siberia with forced labor.

When she was eight, her mother passed away from cholera, and her father died in an accident at work years before. The government sent her to an orphanage from where a priest of the Russian Orthodox Church adopted her to help his wife do the house chores.

She was an outcast partly because of her red hair, considered evil because people associated the color with Judas Iscariot, and because of her Ukrainian background and her religion, a version of Orthodoxy not approved by the one Stalin created in 1942.

Nonetheless, she adapted to her environment. She was athletic and showed exceptional aptitude for learning languages. She mastered the Tartar language of the Siberian natives and the German spoken by deported Volga Germans. In school, a linguistics teacher taught her English.

Her life came to a turning point at thirteen when the priest raped her and chased her out of his house back to the orphanage. The abuse did not stop at the children's home. Fortunately, she befriended an old commissar who recruited her as an informant to keep tabs on the mistrusted Tartars.

At seventeen, he recommended her to the Military Intelligence to study as a Translator, but the GRU decided to train her as an assassin.

Upon graduation, she put her training to use by first poisoning her rapist guardian and then murdering the supervisor who abused her widowed mother.

Her first assignment was to poison the third president of Ukraine with dioxin, to make him sick and disfigured, but not to kill him. She carried out her duties, acting as a waitress, but the deed made her question Butin's character and authority.

She did not mind killing people in the interests of her country. It was her job, and she was good at it, but disfiguring the exceptionally handsome man went against her moral code. To maim a man and remind him of his condition every time he looked in the mirror seemed perverse, an unnecessary cruelty.

Butin

Butin did not want to assassinate the Ukrainian leader because it would have international repercussions. However, he was jealous of the attractive man and wanted to diminish his political appeal.

Nadia saw no necessity or honor in what she did. It was malicious meanness that sowed in her disdain for the vicious administration that reminded her of her childhood tormentors.

Nadia's next job was to track the activities of the American advisor, Manfred, sent to Ukraine by Russia to help elect a pro-Russian thug, Yansin, as the fourth president of Ukraine. She posed as a journalist for RT, a TV propaganda outlet in Moscow, to gain easy access to Ukrainian politicians.

The central election issue concerned the pending Association agreement between the EU and Ukraine that needed the incoming president's signature.

All presidential candidates declared they would sign the document, as did Yansin. However, he would later renege on his election promise because Butin opposed the arrangement, treating Ukraine as if it was still Russia's colony.

The disfigured incumbent was in an intense political tug-of-war with his premier, a charismatic woman who criticized his rule before and during the election campaign. As expected from their infighting, Yansin, who came from industrial Eastern Ukraine, won the three-way contest with nearly 50% of the vote.

Yansin assumed the office and was in power for four years, stalling on the signature while the public clamored for him to approve the document as promised before the election. All Ukrainians wanted to join the EU regardless of whom they voted for.

Nadia was there with a contingent of Russian journalists and spies contemplating whether Butin could persuade Yansin to cheat on his promise. The electorate was in no mood for further procrastination and threatened to throw Yansin out in the upcoming poll.

Knowing that Yansin was a greedy thug, Oleg offered him a bribe to prompt him to dishonor his pledge. He concluded that a personal bribe of $2 billion would be sufficient to make the pawn risk the ire of the public.

When Yansin announced the bribe as a loan and declared he would not approve the Association, the voters became outraged. Two hundred thousand protesters from all over the country gathered in Kyiv, demanding he change his mind and honor the Agreement as promised.

Among the crowd was a young electrician, Orest Korol, who came from the mountainous Carpathian region of Ukraine, the birthplace of Nadia's parents. She admired him because of his unpretentious, polite manner.

Nadia befriended Orest and was with him in a coffee shop for lunch and a chat about the protest. Orest would depart after they ate to a job at a factory while she would stay and wait to meet Manfred's assistant Flannigan and a Russian spy, Klimchuk.

Klimchuk was a loudmouth blowhard who hustled Nadia, but she would have nothing to do with him and often told him to bug off. They would gather to discuss how they should infiltrate the protesters and start a riot that would disrupt the protest by bringing police to come and break it up.

The strategy meeting would have gone smoothly, except the two men came before the couple was through with lunch.

Klimchuk, in his usual boisterous manner, tried to gladhand Nadia to impress his American companion and to show how macho he was, objected to Orest being in there with his presumed girlfriend, saying she ought not to associate with a hohol who was speaking in Ukrainian.

Nadia said her friend had no interest in their meeting and would leave after he finished his drink and meal, and the two should wait at the bar, but Klimchuk insisted Orest depart.

Orest cut the argument short, saying he would go when he was done eating, and refused to move. Klimchuk became belligerent and pushed him off the chair. Orest got up to face his assailant, but Klimchuk brandished a knife.

Nadia interceded.

"Orest, stay out of this. This is not about you. The jerk is trying to impress people. Put down the knife, sit down like a human being, or go to the counter to cool off and wait."

Klimchuk would not heed her warning.

"Fold the knife, or you'll eat it, idiot."

Klimchuk tried to swipe at Orest when Nadia grabbed his arm, flipped him over, and kicked him in the temple. Klimchuk fell unconscious. Nadia took his knife, opened his mouth, and cut the tip of his tongue.

"Next time, sonofabitch, it will be your balls for messing with my friends."

Korol and Nadia departed, not wanting to be involved with the police.

"RT better send someone else to work with me. I don't put up with idiots."

CHAPTER 16

Manfred was an experienced political operative who worked on election campaigns for three former American Republican presidents. Butin hired him to elect his man Yansin as the fourth president of Ukraine so he could thwart the country's pending association with the EU. Later, he would send him to run Doug Trimm's presidential committee in the US.

He commissioned Manfred to organize and guide Yansin's campaign. If he managed to get the pawn elected, he would instruct him to renege on the agreement.

To weaken Ukraine, Oleg wanted to wreck Ukraine's image abroad as a democracy. He sent in several Russian oligarchs to take over the economy of Ukraine, concentrating on its oil and gas business, and use them to sow widespread corruption to condemn Ukraine in the eyes of the West.

Butin's plan worked wonders. Manfred instructed Yansin to promise the electorate he would accept the agreement with the EU. He directed the Russian-owned media to amplify the bitter fight between the incumbent and his premier and persuade the voters to back Yansin as the alternative to both.

There were no viable differences among people in Ukraine for Manfred to exploit in dividing the public. Three centuries of Russian colonial rule did affect the speech in Ukraine, as English did in Ireland and India. However, Ukrainians did not assign much importance to language and spoke a combination of Ukrainian and Russian, referred to as Surzhyk.

They would also not succumb to anti-Semitism or religious division, as became evident when the nation elected a Jew as their president by an unprecedented 70% majority in 2019.

While Yansin's campaign concentrated on the eastern part of Ukraine, thought to be more sympathetic to Russian influence, Moscow's propaganda worked hard to defame the country abroad.

Russian Oligarchs sent a worldwide propaganda blitz about the corruption in Kyiv's government concerning bribes and false accusations of theft of Russian gas crossing Ukraine on its way to the EU. Ukrainians did participate in the questionable deals, as the Kremlin wanted, but the bulk of the fraudulent business in the country was Russian.

Oleg also put his propaganda factories in high gear, spreading lies about Ukraine on the Net to paint the country as a corrupt dictatorship. In reality, Ukrainian was typical of the very definition of a democratic country. Ukraine had highly contested free elections and a peaceful handover of power after every election.

All presidential contests in the country were scrutinized and approved as fair by international monitors and observers.

Butin

Ukraine's presidents won by slim margins in the presence of strong opposition.

Manfred's effort to elect Yansin worked well with the help of Russian-owned propaganda outlets. The shill managed to eke out a 50% majority in the 2010 election to take over the government of Ukraine as the Kremlin's stooge. Following the election, he traveled to Moscow to assure Butin of his loyalty and to get his political instructions.

Like his predecessor, Yansin towered over the diminutive Butin, who resented men of greater physical stature. In his usual petty manner, he made Yansin wait for two hours before he would see him.

His first instruction to Yansin was to dismantle what little army Ukraine had. Butin said the Kremlin signed the *Territorial Integrity of Ukraine* agreement. Thus, all the country needed as a military was a police force loyal to its president.

Butin's second demand was for Yansin to persuade the Rada to extend Russia's rental of its naval base in Crimea. According to the 1991 agreement between Russia and Ukraine, the contract would expire in 2012.

Yansin did as told. The Ukrainian electorate did not mind the lease extension but waited patiently for him to affirm the association of Ukraine with the EU as he promised. By his fourth year in the office, he had to sign or refuse the agreement as it neared expiration.

To ensure Yansin would cheat on his election promise, Butin offered him a personal loan of $2 billion. Yansin accepted the bribe, but his refusal to honor the agreement caused a national outrage. Over two hundred thousand protesters from all over Ukraine descended on Kyiv.

The protests were peaceful and well-mannered, and Orest Korol was among them. Nadia was also there collecting information for the Kremlin.

CHAPTER 17

Nadia invited Orest for dinner at her apartment in Kyiv because they became close friends over the last few months, and she fell in love with him even though she was working against his cause.

He was unaware of her feelings or her profession because she posed as a person sympathetic to the protesters. Despite his attraction to her, he considered her a close friend with shared values and ethnicity. He thought she was an attractive professional woman, always dressed neatly, even in the winter.

She admired him for his honesty and selfless desire to help people. Besides being handsome, Orest was unpretentious and treated Nadia as an equal, a friend who liked her company and never suggested sexual implications because she encouraged none, and he knew she would not tolerate any.

She invited him because she knew trouble was coming and wanted to warn and shield Orest from Butin's henchmen. The protest dragged on for six months, and the Berkut police were now searching for men they said were criminals.

Orest was from a mountain village near where her mother grew up and told her about where her folks came from and the likely family she had there even though she knew nothing about them.

"You have been at the protest since it began. Many protesters leave after a while as new people drift in, yet you are not one of the leaders who will seek political office once this is all over. What made you stay and support this action?" asked Nadia.

"My people have always stood for independent Ukraine, as do yours, although you are from Russia and no longer identify with the mountain folks your parents came from. You have also been here as long as I have.

"You don't go to work as I do to make money and buy food for the camp because you're a Russian. I support the movement because I believe in a democratic government and a sovereign Ukraine.

"You're right that I have no political ambition, and I'm content being an electrician. Since I'm single with no family to support, I spend what I earn buying provisions for the kitchens to stand in solidarity with others who believe in my country.

"Yansin is a traitor. Doesn't he realize that the only way Ukraine will rid itself of Russia and its corrupt, money-grubbing Oligarchs is if Ukraine joins NATO and the European Union?

"Butin tells him what to do, treating him as a puppet. He reneged on his promise to the voters to sign the association with the EU because he took the $2 Billion personal bribe from the Kremlin. The Party of Regions should remove him from office before he destroys our democracy."

"Orest, I don't want you going to the protest tomorrow. I told you I work as an interpreter for a news agency, that is why I'm there all the time. I hear what the foreign reporters say. The journalists expect there will be trouble at the protests.

"The KGB recorded a telephone call of envoy Lund with the US ambassador to Ukraine, speculating about the next election in the country. The conversation was nothing more than a speculation, but Russia seized on it as if America was responsible for the dissent. We expect Moscow will send snipers to kill the protesters."

"God, Nadia, if what you say is true, I must get out there to warn my friends. How do you know this?"

"It's not a secret any longer. The EU press is full of stories, mostly distorted propaganda lies fed by the Kremlin."

"I mean, how did you hear about the assassins?"

"I deduced it knowing what a weasel Butin is. He's a little dictator pretending he's Hitler. It is a natural conclusion, nothing certain yet, although things are getting tense at the camp."

"Still, I better warn my buddies at the soup kitchen."

"Orest, why don't you stay and spend the night with me? You can alert them tomorrow."

"Are you sure? You never indicated you're interested in me that way. We were more like family acquaintances from the mountains."

"You're naive, honest and unpretentious. It's what I like about you. Please stay. I need some loving."

Orest stayed, but the next day, she learned he was shot in the head by a sniper. The leaders of the dissent called for a response, and the movement would get violent.

Nadia did not cry or mourn the passing of her lover. Death was a part of the world she lived in. She just resolved to get even with the Kremlin.

Her defiant family roots were rekindled in her. She took Orest to Carpathian Ukraine, where he came from. To bury him in the grave beside his favorite uncle, Olexa Korol.

She did not stay for the funeral, shed no tears, or get involved in the ritual. To kill the murderer was the only task on her mind, as though it was another assignment.

CHAPTER 18

Yansin was born in Donetsk to a Belorussian father and a Polish mother brought there with Russians to replace the 8 million Ukrainians that Stalin murdered using the forced famine in 1931-32.

He was a thug standing at 6 feet, 6 inches, who started as a small-time criminal apprehended by the police for break-in robbery. His imposing stature propelled him to success. President Kuchma appointed him the prime minister.

Under the guidance of Manfred, he managed to gain 50% of the vote in the fifth democratic election in Ukraine, becoming the country's fourth president. He considered himself a Russian, and before he got in, he did not speak Ukrainian.

After serving for four years, he reneged on his promise to the voters by taking a $2 billion bribe from Butin. The act sparked a wide protest. Not knowing how to handle the dissidents, he sought instruction from his master by sending Manfred, accompanied by the translator Nadia, to Moscow.

Oleg met them in his office in the presence of his drug-smuggling buddy, the mafia chief Igor. After the introduction, the American explained Yansin's plight.

"The president is in a pickle because, after six months, the protest is still going strong. He will certainly lose the next contest if it persists," said Manfred.

"I'm not interested in his well-being or his re-election. I want the dissent to become violent as an excuse for the invasion of Crimea," replied Oleg.

Then, he outlined his plan for solving the protest and annexing Ukraine.

"We will send snipers to shoot the protesters to incite a riot. If Yansin flees the country, it will be my signal to march in and annex Crimea.

"America will not interfere in the annexation despite signing the "Territorial Integrity of Ukraine" agreement. The current president of the US is a cowardly Negro. I will threaten to use nuclear weapons if he intercedes. That will shut him up.

"Igor has a brilliant idea for taking over Crimea. He will form a private army of our soldiers stripped of identity to infiltrate Crimea and occupy the peninsula.

"We will declare Russia has nothing to do with the occupation, pretending the takeover is an act of disgruntled citizens forming an insurgency.

"Yansin will order his military to stand down and not resist the annexation. Afterward, Igor's troops, under the leadership of the commandant of our forces in Transnistria, will invade Luhansk and Donbas.

Butin

"I expect Ukraine to capitulate within a few days. We will absorb it, claiming the Russian Speaking majority in the country wants union with Russia."

Oleg then announced a new task for Manfred.

"Why don't you return to the US to work on electing our man Trimm to the presidency of the US? I hope to use him to dismantle NATO, which stands in the way of my plans for carving out a land corridor to Kaliningrad. How does a salary of $30 million sound?"

The American was not satisfied with the offer because he knew the dictator was after much more than the conquest of Ukraine. Eventually, he wanted to destroy America for causing the demise of his beloved USSR, which Butin considered the greatest tragedy in the annals of history.

"I have long experience as an assistant to former US presidents and to your asset Trimm, who now joined the Republican Party. I propose to become the chairman of his election committee.

"If you send Nadia to the US, she can serve as my contact with you using the propagandist Truson and your bishop Efrem. However, I want my salary to be $60 million, and if I succeed in electing Trimm, I want 100 million more," replied Manfred."

Oleg knew Manfred's service was worth every kopek and agreed to the terms.

To initiate the plan for annexation of Crimea, he would dispatch a group of snipers to Kyiv to take out protest leadership, hoping the dissent would erupt in violence so he could intercede on behalf of the beleaguered Yansin.

Manfred returned to America to chair Trimm's election committee, and Nadia departed to Ukraine with a hundred Russian snipers who were told to begin shooting the dissidents.

Orest was the first victim shot by Konstantin, the leader of the snipers. In response, the protesters rushed the parliament building and sealed off the Russians. The takeover of the Capitol and the killings caused Yansin to flee to Russia. The crowd stormed the assassins and took them as prisoners.

Nadia knew the lives of the killers would be spared by sending them to prison. The idea that the murderer of her lover would live was unacceptable.

Acting as a journalist, she mingled among the dissenters to get access to the captives. She had a bottle of spiked vodka that she slipped to Konstantin with a wink and a smile, knowing he shot Orest. The sniper fell sick with a couple of his friends who shared the drink and died from the poison.

Igor's disguised soldiers, referred to by the West as "the little green men," infiltrated Crimea and took over the region. Yansin ordered the Ukrainian military to stay in their barracks and not oppose Russians, saying he asked for their help in subduing the revolution. The takeover was completed in weeks with only a few fatalities.

Butin was delighted with Igor's success and instructed him to form a contingent of mercenaries as his private army to attack the Donbas and the Luhansk regions in the eastern parts of Ukraine, intending to annex the rest of Ukraine.

However, with the traitor out of the country, impeached by his party, the Ukrainians began to fight back, and the citizens of Kharkiv and Mariupol, acting on their own, chased out the invaders with nothing but spades in their hands.

After Ukraine regained a considerable portion of the seized territory, the conflict turned into a seven-year frozen war between Ukrainian forces and Igor's mercenaries named "Wolfgang" to imitate the German stormtroopers.

Moscow declared the occupied parts of the two regions independent republics, but nobody recognized them except Russia.

Nadia's next assignment was to go to the Nevsky monastery to be trained as a novice to accompany bishop Efrem as the representative of the Stalinist Church to the World Ecumenical Council in the US.

Killing Konstantin for murdering her lover was not enough. She decided to serve as a double agent and offered her service to the FBI informant Father Semyon of St. Nicholas Orthodox Church.

Nadia became the conduit between Manfred and the Kremlin and an informant on the activities of Truson and Trimm's political organization to the priest.

It was not about disloyalty to Russia as far as she was concerned. It was vengeance for the death of the only man she would ever love and give herself to as a sweetheart. Orest was more than a lover to her. He was the link to her roots, a voice to her inner soul.

CHAPTER 19

Doug Trimm was the son of a wealthy real estate developer whose wealth fueled his ambition in business and politics. Despite being a mediocre student, with the support of his dad's finances, he launched multiple commercial ventures, some successful, others resulting in several bankruptcies.

His many deals with securing government-backed loans, often exposed as illegal, made him bitter toward the federal agencies and regulators and produced in him a deep-seated hatred that drove him to seek revenge by undermining the American democratic system.

His political activity began with presidential runs, ignored or laughed at until he succeeded as a TV celebrity. The exposure to public entertainment gave him the name recognition of more than just another rich man, but his first attempt as an independent candidate for the White House met swift failure.

However, when he switched to the Republican party, Butin saw in him an ally he would manipulate to support his desire to resurrect Russia's Empire through territorial conquests of its neighbors. Trimm was his old friend, having visited him on many occasions since the collapse of the USSR.

To help Trimm's presidential ambition, Oleg employed numerous former US officials, grooming them as potential supporters of Trimm's bid for the 2016 US presidency. Their endorsement with massive Russian propaganda gained Doug popularity among conservative voters and Evangelicals, which led to his confirmation as the GOP nominee.

Following his nomination, he embarked on a caustic campaign of slurs and denigration of his Democratic opponent. His controversial stand on social issues polarized the nation, and his anti-government rhetoric encouraged street demonstrations radicalizing the nation.

To ensure Trimm's success, Butin persuaded his influential American friends to recommend his man, Manfred, as the chairman of the Republican Election Committee.

Manfred was an experienced strategist who would provide his boss with well-disguised contact using Nadia and Truson as informants.

The nun fed the newscaster propaganda Russia designed to divide America's voters, targeting gays and transgender people, demonizing them similar to fascist attacks vilifying the Jews.

However, Manfred knew that division of the public required more than the abuse of scapegoats. He needed a symbol akin to the Nazi swastika, which would rally people to Trimm's cause.

Butin

He chose a red farmer's hat with the slogan MAGA, meaning Make America Great Again, written on it to differentiate Doug's followers from the liberals dubbed "commies."

Trimm's stand against homosexuals and his support of the anti-abortion movement endeared him to the leader Fallworth, who endorsed him as his choice for the next president of the US.

In an evenly divided electorate, Fallworth's evangelical community could tip the result in favor of Trimm.

The communication between Manfred and Butin through their informants was inefficient. He needed to meet with the dictator personally to plan their action in promoting Trimm's election. Nadia accompanied Manfred to the get-together as an interpreter.

At the meeting, Oleg promised Manfred to devote thousands of bloggers to generate misinformation about the democratic candidate. He would direct Russia's hackers to break into the records of US government Institutions to dig up dirt on her and discredit any damning information about Trimm, such as his visits with prostitutes.

The Russian intelligence agency, the FSB, would forward any negative information about her to the FBI using the Danish whistleblower, who had a reputation as an honest source of political wrongdoing.

Nadia told Semyon about Manfred's meeting with Butin and the hacking efforts. The priest passed the information to the bureau.

When the FBI confronted Trimm with the knowledge about Manfred communicating with the Kremlin, implying he was colluding with Russia, Doug dismissed the charge as falsehood. Still, he had to fire his chairman.

Angered by the implication of conspiracy, Trimm trashed the FBI along with the US Military establishment and said no collusion took place between him and Moscow.

To counter the accusation, he asked the FSB in a TV show to find dirt on his Democratic female opponent.

Kremlin's hackers took up the request, broke into the US network of servers, and found that while she was the Secretary of State, she stored her emails on her private server.

The documents were insignificant, but the fact some had the word "classified" stamped on them made the News outlets label her as a person negligent with US secrets.

Truson played up the importance of the emails on his evening talk shows, implying America would not be safe in the hands of the "crooked" Democrat woman.

Despite the Kremlin's disinformation efforts, surveys indicated the Democrats would win the 2016 contest, and much to Butin's chagrin, his intense propaganda campaign on behalf of Trimm appeared less effective than he had hoped.

Butin

However, the FSB came up with a brilliant last-minute plan. They repackaged her old emails as new ones and passed them to the unsuspecting Dane, who asked the FBI to announce the recent find the day before the election.

The deception tipped the poll in Trimm's favor because it could not be answered in time.

Butin was overjoyed with the success and held a congratulatory champagne party in Doug's honor. Oleg had his man in the White House. Things were looking up for his plans to revive the Russian Empire. Flattery would ensure Trimm was on board with the Kremlin's agenda.

CHAPTER 20

The Kremlin groomed Trimm as its ally for over thirty years, starting with the waning of the USSR. Trimm adored Butin and visited him several times. Now that Doug became America's President, Butin was eager to meet with his admirer.

Trimm did not speak Russian despite his many visits to Russia and the fact his wife spoke the language.

Butin required a GRU interpreter who would not raise suspicions at his meeting with Trimm and his entourage in Germany. Nadia fit the bill perfectly. She had been to the US and was above suspicion because she served as a novice of bishop Efrem.

Nevsky monastery informed her she was being recalled to Moscow to serve as Butin's translator in his pending meeting with President Trimm at the G20 meeting.

Although the journalists would attend the general meeting, she was the only one who would be present and wired to record the one-on-one meeting between the two leaders.

Before she departed for Russia, she went to her usual Sunday mass to tell Father Semyon he would lose her as his informant on Efrem's and Truson's activities.

The priest suggested they could visit after the service. They could sit on the bench reserved for the weak elderly parishioners and talk openly rather than meet in the confessional booth. There were no other seats. St. Nicholas was an old-style Orthodox Church. The faithful stood praying, like the Jews.

"I'm sorry you're leaving. You have been my friend, not just a member of my congregation. I will miss our discussions. Although you're not a nun, I always felt you were a devout believer."

"Father, you are correct in thinking I believe there is something in the Universe besides this world and the stars, but I am an agnostic, unsure if I will take my vows. I doubt Resurrection as the apostle Thomas did because I need to verify the reality.

"I do not subscribe to the beliefs of religion founded on miracles. I do not need an intermediary between me and God if one exists. I keep my beliefs to myself and do not force them on others or accept the beliefs they want to impose on me."

"Nadia, you are a gifted person with no need for comfort that religion and belief in God provide to those who are not as independent as you or have problems they cannot cope with on their own and need the support religion offers.

"We, as the servants of God, provide more than religious dogma. We provide ease of mind to those facing hard times with reality every day. Church has a social as well as spiritual obligation to the faithful."

"I am curious, Father, why do you betray your religion by informing on bishop Efrem?"

"You should know why I report on Efrem's evil plans to the FBI. As you told me, Efrem is a spy. He serves the State, not God. We, the Orthodox Christians in America, are the descendants of the original czarist Patriarchy.

"We were here before the Bolsheviks exterminated our clergy in the USSR. The informant organization Stalin created and dressed in clerical attire is the abomination of Christianity together with the shills Efrem and Onufry, the Patriarch of all Russia.

"We are tied to them only for the sake of the unity of the Faithful and the financial support we get from the Kremlin. You can see our sparse congregation is not enough to sustain our existence.

"Since you brought up my loyalty, why are you betraying the Motherland?"

"First, let me say we both know about the informant agency, the Moscow Patriarchy, and my part of that deception. I am not proud of it."

Though he probably suspected it, Nadia did not want Father Semyon to know she was GRU. This was not their usual conversation in a confessional booth. This was a discussion between friends.

"I was an orphan when I was eight, and I lived among bad people and associated with evil ones all my life until I found my angel Orest.

"After my parents died, I became a ward of a priest who repeatedly raped me, and when I turned to the authorities for help, he cast me out to an orphanage where I was beaten and taught to cheat and lie to survive.

"I never knew a decent person before I met him at the Maidan protest, where I posed as a journalist but served as an FSB informant.

"He thought I was a writer and offered me a fresh apple he picked off a tree, never wanting anything from me, not even a polite conversation.

"He was there not because of political activism. He thought it was wrong for the President to take a bribe from Butin and renege on the promise to the voters to be elected.

"He thought it was indecent to deceive people and came to Kyiv from the Carpathian Mountains to support the protesters by buying them food.

"We fell in love after I befriended him, and he never asked for my affection in return for his. He loved someone he thought I was, and perhaps I could have been that person if my folks had not died at an early age.

"I tried to shield him from harm by asking Butin's chief assassin not to kill him, but he did anyway. He murdered more than my lover on that day. He also extinguished any decency I had left in my rotten life. Orest was innocent and paid with his life for being kind.

"I will see to it that the rot that destroys our nation comes to an end because Russian people should live free like they do here, without fear and the ever-present apprehension Russians have that their neighbor will betray them.

"People in Russia are scared to speak about politics in front of their children lest their kids repeat what they heard to a priest or a teacher who will report them to the FSB.

"Then, the police would haul them away to some god-forsaken place in the Siberian Taiga. The children would never see their folks again, thinking the parents did something wrong.

"The protesters wanted nothing more than freedom and association with the EU where Ukrainians could live as free people as the politicians promised before the election.

"Russia had no right to invade their country and take Crimea from them. The Kremlin betrayed its pledge to respect the territorial integrity of Ukraine, as did the US and Britain. The world is rotten, and America is headed there with people like Trimm and Truson."

"Why are you being transferred, and what will you do once you return to Moscow?"

Butin

"I have decided to become a correspondent like my love thought I was. I can work as a translator and hope to return to the US as an embassy employee after I see Patriarch Onufry and explain to him my decision."

I cannot live as a free person in Russia, and I need to come back to take down that treacherous sonofabitch Truson rotting America to its core, she thought.

CHAPTER 21

Nadia went to the headquarters to get instructions for her assignment. She would serve as Oleg Butin's translator. He was fluent in German and understood enough English to know whether she translated his comment accurately.

The protocol demanded he speak in Russian at the meeting attended by the journalists but not at his one-on-one meeting with Trimm.

At their first meeting with Butin, Trimm had his interpreter and the Secretary of State present. Nadia sat beside Butin as he began the conversation.

"Let me congratulate you again on being elected as the president of the US. I have been following your campaign and think you performed brilliantly."

Butin continued the flattery, and Doug was lapping it up like a schoolboy.

"Cooperation between our two countries will allow us to solve problems in troubled spots and benefit the world."

"Thank you for your confidence we will have good economic and political understanding. The press in America has been concerned with Russia's interference in our election. Could you clarify this issue to address their concern?"

Butin

"Let me assure you, the Russian Federation had no involvement in the American electoral process. Of course, we followed your campaign since you are the dominant economy in the world. I guarantee we had no hand in your country's internal affairs.

"Your preceding administration made a mess in the Middle East, and both Russia and the government of Turkey are opposed to the establishment of a Kurdish state in the region. Why do we need to fracture Syria now that the Kurds have defeated ISIS?"

"The person who held my position had a socialist mindset and lacked an understanding of what the world needs. Let me say he was not even qualified to be America's president because he was not born in the US. He had no experience in economy and business and was ignorant about foreign affairs, as you saw when you took over Crimea."

"No American heads of state had the wisdom and your knowledge of economics. As an outstanding businessman, you are the most successful self-made billionaire I have ever met.

"I am sure we will improve our economies if we work together. As a sign of our willingness to cooperate with you, we have decided not to retaliate against your predecessor's sanctions. We hope you will lift them because you understand better than anyone it is in our mutual interest."

"You know, I do not have the free hand as you do to end the restrictions, but I will do my best to do away with them. We do not need to put blocks in the way of our businesses.

"The Sanctions came about because of Crimea, but I think you had every right to annex Crimea. You told me before, during my many visits to Russia, that Crimea is vital to Russian defense and its Naval presence in Europe."

"You have keen insight into world affairs, and I appreciate your understanding of our position towards Ukraine."

"Oleg, I do not believe in the proliferation of useless states as happened after the dissolution of the USSR, and I do not subscribe to our participation in NATO.

"It is an outdated military alliance siphoning off our money. The EU should pay for its defense, not America, or at least bear the fair share of its cost, which I will insist on.

"The European countries must have their means to protect themselves instead of depending on the United States for defense."

"You are correct, Doug. The EU is an economic conglomeration of many states. It does not need political unity or common defense directed against our country. I give you my word we are no danger to the EU.

"We had an agreement at the breakup of the Communist Empire that NATO would not expand eastward. We think NATO is a threat to Russia because it expanded close to our border when it incorporated the Warsaw Pact Countries after the USSR dissolved.

"The collapse of the Soviet Union was the greatest tragedy the world has ever seen, and the expansion of NATO was unwarranted. Don't you agree, President Trimm?"

"The world was much more stable when the USSR and America were the dominant military powers. We had fewer borders to worry about, and our relations were defined clearly."

He eats out of my hand. I can't wait to meet him alone so we can decide what we will do, thought Butin.

When the meeting ended, Trimm insisted his translator gave up his notes, and others present there would keep its content secret. Trimm thought he had the Russian's respect and understanding, deceived as he was by the flattery.

CHAPTER 22

Trimm met with Butin without any interpreter on the American side, and Nadia was there more as a source of proper words than a translator.

However, she wore a listening device to record the whole conversation as evidence the Kremlin might need to persuade Trimm to abide by their agreement. The FSB also had the previously collected golden shower tapes in case it needed more persuasive means to make him cooperate with Moscow.

The meeting wound up more as a list of instructions Oleg had for Trimm than an exchange of ideas.

Doug said he admired and appreciated how the FSB provided the FBI with phony new emails the agency made public the day before the election. It was a master stroke of deception that swung the vote in his favor. He marveled at Oleg's absolute control of Russia and wished he could do so in America.

Oleg first replied regarding the email ruse by stating most people are dolts (Nadia corrected him by saying people are susceptible) because a well-placed lie at the right time is far more effective in prompting people to action than the truth.

Butin

As for his control of the country, he said it was natural. Russians have always had a strongman dictatorship ruled by fear. The harsher the ruler, the more people loved and feared him, as demonstrated by Stalin.

Oleg told Trimm it would be much harder for him to control America because the US is an entrenched Democracy. However, he could do as Hitler had by having a well-organized faction like the brown shirts take over in an evenly divided, indecisive government.

Butin pointed out that democracy is inefficient and prone to willful disregard of the state's interests by its oligarchs, as was the case in Maximov's attempted democracy in Russia.

Oleg had to tear down his predecessor's democratic rule by subduing the oil barons who drained the country of funds by hoarding their wealth in the EU and Britain. Some had to be jailed, while others committed suicide. He winked as he voiced his last statement.

He continued by saying Dictatorships have been the natural form of government since time immemorial. Of course, in the olden days, they were Kings ruling by Divine right. Now, rulers cannot be that bold.

Patriarch Alexy II, whom Butin assassinated to appoint Onufry, wanted to anoint Butin as the Divine czar, like the czars before the Bolshevik revolutions. Being of German descent, Oleg fit the bill perfectly, but he knew that after eighty years of State-enforced Atheism, the people would no longer buy the notion of him as a heavenly ruler.

Instead, he fashioned the Russian Federation as Russia's Fourth Reich because Hitler had the correct idea to rule as a supreme leader by the people's choice.

Russia would succeed, whereas Hitler failed because he set out to conquer the world. Butin wanted only to regain territories the czars had before WW I.

Nowadays, people do not accept celestial rulers, so dictators create a make-believe legislature to disguise the only real God, the strong man with the power of life and death, over the dull masses.

The deception is necessary because modern society wants to think that people are in charge, and at the same time, they want their leader to care for and feed them.

Present-day kings have to call themselves presidents. They stage false elections to control the proletariat and portray their countries as something other than the fascist dictatorships they are.

As a totalitarian country, Russia used disguise for decades to create an image of itself that the Kremlin wishes the world to believe rather than what it is because familiarity breeds defiance and contempt.

This was true during Muscovy, Czarist Russia, Communist Russia, and Russia's Fourth Reich.

Butin

Trimm said that, unlike dictatorship, a free society invented and innovated and was responsible for society's progress. His business experience in the housing and entertainment industry showed Democracies prefer to rule over prosperous people.

Butin replied that innovation works up to a point and needs to be controlled. Technology does not necessarily improve the quality of life. Americans were no better off today than in the sixties. Furthermore, prosperity encourages dissent and chaos. Russia does not need it.

Butin then turned to advise Trimm about his presidency.

The US should stop pushing for global freedom and democracy because the world does not want it. Most people care only if their bellies are full and their sex is satisfied. The ambitious will always rise to the top by any means possible, including crime, as Trimm has.

To rule America like a strong man, Doug needed to end America's activity abroad and concentrate on dismantling its current system. He did not need to abolish the institutions of the government. He only needed to transform them into the tools he could use to govern the masses.

He was also advised to form a militia group similar to Wolfgang to subdue objectors to his takeover.

Above all, to be a dictator, Trimm needed to create a scapegoat minority to rally supporters to his side. Migrants were his best choice as scapegoats because they were least able to defend themselves.

As for America's foreign policy, he needed to make peace with the religious fanatics in Afghanistan because the people who ran the government did not believe in the American system imposed on them.

Afghan men, regardless of whether they served the government or the warlords, aimed to maintain their control over women. It is what their religion is all about. They wished to sell girls like sheep.

Oleg predicted that as soon as America pulled out, the Afghan government would collapse within days because people in the government believed in the same values as the insurgents.

The conflict in Syria was different. ISIS wanted more than dominance over Syria. The fanatics sought to dominate the whole Middle East. If they were to succeed, they would threaten the global economy as they would control much of the world's oil supply.

Butin said Trimm's inept predecessor made one sensible move by arming the Kurds, but letting them form their state was wrong. It would fracture Syria and create yet another useless state as the collapse of the USSR did.

Besides, the Turkish president opposed a Kurdish state in Syria, fearing it could encourage separatism by Kurds in eastern Turkey.

The last point brought Butin to the purpose of the meeting. It concerned NATO. He said Russia needed a land corridor to the Kaliningrad enclave and the control of Ukraine's Black Sea ports.

Russia had to regain Ukraine as an integral part of the Kremlin's territory. This is not only due to its economic significance and skilled labor force but also because, without Ukraine, the world perceives Russia as an oil-rich country rather than an empire.

Oleg asked Doug to disband NATO, not because the organization was a threat to Russia but because NATO stood in the way of the Russian conquest of Ukraine and its plan to carve out a land passage to Kaliningrad through Lithuania.

Trimm replied he could deliver on Afghanistan and Syria but not on disbanding NATO. Not until he secured control over the Courts and the government institutions. That alone would keep him busy his first four years.

He would pressure the EU countries to pay their fair share of the cost of NATO and the housing of American troops in the EU.

The EU members might decide the increased expense for NATO is not worth the security it provides and withdraw their membership as France had done in the past.

Doug promised that in his second term, he would abandon NATO because national defense organizations would not object since he would control them.

When the meeting ended, Oleg asked Nadia if she recorded the conversation. She replied that the listening device was on but did not reveal that she taped it at her friend's place and the GRU headquarters.

Trimm promptly delivered on his agreement about negotiating with the Afghan insurgents. He bypassed the established pseudo-democratic government that later collapsed, as Butin predicted.

Trimm also betrayed the Kurds, America's boots on the ground. As an excuse, he said Turkey objected to the establishment of a Syrian Kurdish state. Kurds had nowhere to turn and accepted Russian control over most of Syria's territory.

NATO countries grudgingly agreed to increased financial support for NATO but did not leave the organization as Trimm hoped.

Doug did manage to load the courts with his sympathizers, but the judiciary was always unpredictable because their appointments were for life.

Butin

He cultivated the allegiance of far-right groups who would rally to take over the government if he lost the next election.

The next time, Trimm met Butin in Finland where he informed Oleg he would not deliver on NATO disbandment as promised because if he did, polls indicated he could lose his bid for the second term.

In response, Butin advised him to seize power if his opponent won. However, to take control, he would need the support of the army.

Oleg said Trimm should stop trashing the American Military Establishment. While dismantling the US intelligence agencies was the correct step, denigration of the Generals was not. Any attempt at seizing the government would fail without their backing.

Butin said he was not ready to invade Ukraine until 2022 and hoped Trimm would be re-elected and NATO would be disbanded so he would have a free hand at reconquering the USSR's former territory.

To accomplish the defeat of Ukraine, Butin would rely on brainwashing the Russian masses by labeling Ukrainians as Nazis, like Hitler's troops.

First, he would attack Kyiv and the eastern regions of Ukraine, where the population spoke a version of Russian mixed with Ukrainian, hoping the locals would welcome the

Russian invasion because they identified with Russia, not Ukraine.

CHAPTER 23

Nadia returned to Nevsky Monastery to get her assignment. She was apprehensive about meeting Onufry. She hid her recorder inside her jacket she left at her friend's place.

The coat was not where she left it, so she did not know if her friend saw it and ignored it or reported it to the KGB. The conversation between Trimm and Butin was not on the instrument. So it was either erased, or the device failed to turn on. She would figure out which was the case from her new assignment.

The patriarch was in his usual comfortable attire when she came to see him.

"How are you, comrade?"

Talking like a communist, he asked if she wanted a shot of single malted scotch.

"I'll pass on the drink, your eminence."

I don't want to befriend the old bastard by drinking with him, but I will know I am safe if he sends me back to the United States. I will be in mortal danger if my assignment is in the Russian Federation. The orders come down from Butin, who decides life and death.

The fact he offered her a drink did not mean she was safe. Being the only one privy to the secret conversation between the two presidents, Oleg, suspicious as he was of everybody, might well decide to assassinate the sole witness. For now, she seemed safe because of the offer of a drink.

"The Supreme leader wants you to return to your job in the Ecumenical Christian Council in the US, but with an added duty to spy on Efrem, he may defect as he has no family in Russia."

I don't have any either, so what do they think of me?

"You can take the next flight to New York with our representative to the UN."

"Splendid, I'm sure I'll be leaving. I'll have that drink of scotch if you don't mind."

Onufry poured her a stiff shot that she downed in one gulp as she walked out and sighed with relief. Her fate would be different if he reassigned her to a job in Russia. The authorities trusted her, at least for now.

She arrived in the US disappointed. She hoped to have a record of Trimm's meeting with Butin, to hand it over to Semyon, but all she had now was her word.

Efrem welcomed her back. He complained that Trimm lost re-election, and his attempt to take over the government by force failed because the US Military refused to side with him. Exactly what Oleg predicted would happen if the army did not back Doug.

Butin

The bishop said he was not surprised with the outcome of the MAGA insurrection because the rabble that attacked the Capitol was pathetic and disorganized.

Trimm's false claim that the polls were rigged had only one outcome: it was what Butin had wanted. It discredited democracy. Kremlin could now claim the elections in America were no better than in any third-world banana republic.

On the following Sunday, Nadia offered to help Father Semyon with his preparations for Easter so she could talk with him about what she heard at the G20 meeting in Germany.

The priest suggested she meet his contact, but she thought the idea was too dangerous. Instead, she asked him to tell his handler that Russia's war against Ukraine was imminent and would begin next year when Butin would be ready to invade the country.

The result of Semyon's report to the FBI was predictable. The Father could not reveal his source because it would lead to the nun. The agency thought his information came from St George's parishioner who worked at the Russian embassy and discarded the account about the invasion as unreliable.

Since Nadia was on her assignment as the interpreter, she stopped serving as the go-between Moscow News and the influencer Truson, who now got his instruction from a consulate employee.

He still asked her for sexual favors, but she would not meet him anyplace other than Fallworth's regular ecumenical meetings with Efrem. She realized the FSB operatives would be watching her because she knew the content of the secret meeting at G20.

Satisfied with having nothing to do with Truson, she still wanted to expose him to his employer as a pervert and traitor to the US. The newsman disgusted her.

During their encounters, unknown to him, she filmed their liaisons to use as evidence at a later date to take down the treacherous hypocrite who claimed he was a devout Christian and a family man. Their relationship was always on her terms. After their first encounter, he never tried to force himself on her again.

If she sought direct contact with the owner of the Christian News Company, it would arouse FSB's suspicion. She had to wait for an opportunity to take down the worm.

Truson did not disguise his association with Russia any longer, and communicated directly with the Russian propaganda outlets that reprinted his tirades about Ukraine and the American election. The FSB persuaded him to announce that someone hacked the voting machines, altering the results of the polls against Trimm.

The press publicized the outright lie that MAGA supporters used to discredit the electoral process.

Butin

The manufacturer of the machines sued Christian News for billions of dollars in damage. The news Company would have to pay millions to the plaintiff if they lost the legal case.

At the end of the litigation, the news agency lost and paid hundreds of thousands for damaging the manufacturer's reputation.

However, Truson remained in his job because the public kept his ratings at an all-time high. His fortune changed when Efrem asked Nadia to serve as an interpreter at a meeting between the Russian ambassador to the US and the chief of Christian News.

The meeting concerned Russia's threat to invade Ukraine by massing three hundred thousand troops on the Ukrainian border and because Truson advocated Butin's invasion of Ukraine on the company's evening show. The diplomat needed to clarify Russia's pending attack on Ukraine to the American news media.

The interview was in the company conference room, where it would be televised. Nadia arrived early, waiting for the two guests to arrive. The owner entered first. Greeting him with a handshake, she placed an evidence flash drive in his hand as she said quietly.

"This is for your information, sir. I hope you will not betray me."

The owner did not let on what happened, keeping a deadpan expression.

"I'm glad to meet you. How did you learn English so well?"

"I worked as a nanny for an American family in Moscow when I was young." lied Nadia.

She hoped he would not betray his source and that she was not watched, but that was not the case because a Russian journalist saw that she passed on the USB.

The owner did not betray her, but he showed the record to Truson and fired him. He said he would expose Truson's sexual escapades if he did not go quietly.

The newscaster informed the FSB why his boss sacked him. The official reason for losing his job was the loss of the suit filed by the voting machine manufacturer and the fact that Truson badmouthed the owner.

Using what Truson said and what the journalist observed, the FSB concluded Nadia was the snitch and put out an assassination order against her.

The FBI learned of the assassination plan, and Father Semyon warned her life was in danger. She had no choice but to run. The FSB would find her no matter where she fled. She decided her safest place was in Ukraine, among people fighting for survival.

CHAPTER 24

Igor was Butin's childhood friend, unconditionally loyal to his schoolmate. He disliked how his buddy disguised himself as the elected president and Russia as a democracy instead of admitting it was a totalitarian State as Hitler's Germany was.

As far as he was concerned, a supreme leader should not care what the rest of the world thought about him. Stalin and Hitler were his idols because they did not hide being dictators and killing people.

However, Igor valued loyalty above all else and overlooked Oleg's deception. He just wished his childhood friend was more honest and less petty.

Russia was on the verge of invading Ukraine, so he called his trusted lieutenant Boris to discuss their plans for the impending war. They needed to recruit more people for their part in the upcoming assault.

They were tasked with attacking Ukrainians from Donbas using their supposedly private troops. The territory was captured in a prior attack on Ukraine in 2014 after they invaded Crimea with Russia's army stripped of its identity.

The disguise in the Crimean invasion gave them the idea of forming Wolfgang, a voluntary military organization of Igor billed as a warlord. The deception allowed the Kremlin to deny involvement in territorial conquest in Ukraine and its support of dictators in Syria and Africa.

Boris said Butin's intrusion abroad spread Wolfgang's forces too thin. He should have confined his conquests to the countries adjacent to Russia by establishing a land corridor to Kaliningrad and Crimea.

To alleviate the thinning of their force, Igor suggested they could look for volunteers in the newly occupied territories in Syrians and Libya, as well as in traditional vassal States like Serbia. Some Russians were reluctant to volunteer because Ukrainians were their comrades in WWII.

Boris thought another source of conscripts for the mercenary army could come from the prisons and migrants from the former Asian republics of the USSR.

Igor said it was a sound idea, but they should distinguish between the original soldiers of fortune in Wolfgang and the prisoners. The bona fide troops prided themselves on pretending they were German-style stormtroopers and would object to being lumped with convicts.

Igor joked that the invasion would accomplish two things besides conquering Ukraine. It would kill off Russia's indigenous Siberian population and rid the society of criminals.

Boris replied, saying Russia would never be short of felons and perverts because its most prominent government officials and leaders were both.

The regular Russian army would invade Ukraine from Belarus against Kyiv and Kharkiv. In the initial assault on two cities, the campaign would deploy the Asians of Siberia and Chechens from the Caucasus. If the conflict lasted longer than a few days, the two non-Slavic groups would be used in human wave attacks as cannon fodder.

However, the Military Hierarchy predicted Ukraine would capitulate within a week. Igor and Boris did not buy the optimistic scenarios. Their experience from serving on the front lines in Donbas after its occupation in 2014 told them the Ukrainians would not quit fighting after a couple of days.

They thought the war would be a prolonged struggle and most likely become a guerrilla war. The conflict would last for many years, as it did in Afghanistan for the Soviets and the Americans.

However, the world thought Ukraine was an easy mark for Russia's conquest and would collapse in 48 hours. It was poorly armed with no immediate help from NATO or its neighbors. Some, such as Hungary, would side with the Russians rather than the Ukrainians.

The historical animosity toward Ukraine by its neighbors dates back to 1921 when all neighbors attacked the Ukrainian state established by the 1919 Paris Accord after WWI. Each neighbor wanted to get a piece of Ukraine's territory. Russia and Poland managed to occupy most of the country, but all its neighbors got their share of the land of the Ukrainian people who lived there for centuries.

At the time, the central countries of Europe craved colonies to emulate the territorial greatness of Western Europeans. Pieces of Ukraine satisfied that need.

CHAPTER 25

Butin convened a meeting to discuss his plan of attack on Ukraine with his military leaders, including Igor and Boris, who led the campaign to annex Crimea and invade parts of Donbas in 2014.

The Army Chief of Staff suggested Oleg wait to invade until after Trimm again became the president of the US in 2024 because Doug would not aid Ukraine.

The second in command disagreed, saying the time for the invasion was optimal now because Ukraine was ill-equipped. It had shoulder-fired weapons and old Soviet-era tanks his men would quickly destroy.

Boris interjected it was too late to invade Ukraine because the planners committed a dire mistake in 2014. Following the annexation of Crimea, they should have initiated an all-out assault on unarmed Ukraine. Trimm's predecessor would have done nothing about the invasion other than verbally condemn the Kremlin as he did then.

Boris continued by saying the missed opportunity to conquer all of Ukraine in 2014 gave them time to unite. The Ukrainians will be a formidable foe if America supplies them with modern weapons and an air force. The current President of America condemned Russia's invasion when he was the VP. He promised if elected, he would arm Ukraine to repel any future incursions by Moscow.

The Marshal countered Ukraine would collapse overnight in front of the overwhelming Russian might. Every expert suggested it would. He doubted America, threatened by Russia with nuclear war, would help Ukraine. Even if it did, it would be too little and too late. He predicted any resistance to the assault on Kyiv would vanish in days. NATO would do nothing in response other than impose more meaningless sanctions.

Boris scoffed at the Chief's comment, stating he did not understand the character of the Ukrainian people. The Chief never lived among them. They were the proud grandsons of the men who bore the brunt of the fight at Stalingrad. They would not be defeated as quickly as everybody hoped.

He contended they would be fierce opponents. The best Russia could hope for is if their current president, a Jew, capitulated under nuclear threats rather than be deposed.

The commanding general asked if the Russian soldiers would be motivated to fight the brotherly Ukrainians. He recalled many Russians refused to fight during the first

Chechen war because the Chechens were fellow Soviets. Why would they now fight against their other compatriots?

The chief propagandist at the gathering replied he had the answer. Every conquest needs a slogan to generate hate to motivate people to fight. Otherwise, why would anyone attack someone who did them no harm? Ukrainians never harmed Russia. To condition Russians to assault them, his propaganda factories would spread on the Net the falsehood Ukrainians are Nazis.

The slander would transfer to Russians the hatred they have for Hitler. Some Western Ukrainians, whose fathers served in the Austrian army in WWI, sided with the Germans in WWII.

Igor asked who would believe the propagandist's absurdity that Ukrainians, former Soviet compatriots, were Nazis? The propagandist replied his experience showed that the lie repeated a thousand times in a closed press environment becomes the truth because nobody can counter the lies.

The motive for the war would be advertised as the liberation of Russian Speakers in the East from the evil fascists of the West. Those people were ambivalent about their nationality. They would meet the invading troops with flowers, proclaiming Russians as their liberators.

Boris, who fought against eastern Ukrainians in Donbas, dismissed the propagandist's naive comments, saying he lived in a dreamland. People in Ukraine never cared about who spoke Russian or Ukrainian and used a mixture of both languages, often referred to as Surzhyk.

The occupation they suffered for three hundred years affected their language as colonialism did elsewhere. It did not change the loyalty people had for their country and the love of their nation.

He ridiculed the idea the so-called Russian Speakers would bring flowers to greet the invading Russians as a wishful dream. Instead, they would bear guns to resist the invades. Any notion they were loyal to Russia because of their Russian speech was a fallacy, believed only by propagandists.

Butin became furious with Boris for his statements. Oleg maintained there was no such thing as the Ukrainian nation or Ukraine as a State. In his mind, Ukrainians were Russian people, and Ukraine was just a province of Russia. He vented his anger by accusing Boris of incompetence and threatened to put him in jail.

To discredit him, Butin mentioned the fact Boris shot down a Dutch passenger plane in 2014, killing over three hundred people, a misjudgment that resulted in the condemnation of Russia even though the Kremlin blamed the Ukrainian army for the incident.

The accusation was false. He was not responsible for the fiasco. Boris did not reply but knew Gorkov was the one who downed the civilian aircraft.

Following the tirade, Butin explained the justification for the proposed invasion:

"Everyone thought Ukraine was a part of the Russian Empire. This perception convinced the people of Russia and the rest of the world that Kyiv was essential to Russia's status as a global power. Russia was just another oil-rich country without Ukraine, not an Imperial Might.

"After Peter the Great conquered Ukraine and changed the name of Muscovy to Russia, we also assumed the heritage of Ukraine. Two countries can't claim identical origin and history. Ukraine, as the region of Russia, makes the history of Kyivan Rus our history," concluded Butin.

Butin proclaimed conquering Ukraine would reinstate Russia as a superpower by reclaiming the legacy of Czar Peter and Stalin.

The meeting culminated with an agreement that Russia would attack Ukraine with three hundred thousand troops. It would cut off Kyiv and Kharkiv, Ukraine's two largest cities, from the rest of the country. At the same time, Wolfgang's army would push westward from Donbas to create a land bridge to Crimea.

Following the decision, Butin issued an executive order to prepare transport trucks and railways to remove all grain from Ukraine. He resolved to starve the population like Stalin did when he killed eight million Ukrainians in 1931-32. He contended that starving people do not rebel only look for food to survive.

After the meeting, Igor pulled Butin aside to air his thoughts.

"You can always count on my unquestioned loyalty, just like when we were kids. I know these people because I have fought them after we invaded Crimea. They are proud and will not back down. I am sure NATO will eventually supply them with weapons. The conflict will turn into a guerrilla war like Afghanistan."

"That is why I'm going to starve them and send in a million men to occupy the country and subdue them. I intend to wipe Ukrainians off the face of the Earth and erase Ukraine from the map of the world. History of Russia will proclaim me as the restorer of Russia's dignity. Don't voice such doubts or heresy to me again," said Butin.

I'll kill you if you contradict me again, thought Butin.

Butin

You are fooling yourself, but I'll wait for the result. You know nothing except wishful propaganda claiming they are Russian. For three hundred years, they refused to call themselves anything other than Ukrainians, thought Igor.

It turned out Igor was right. The war went on for years. Ukrainians came out as one to face the invaders, and Nadia was there fighting alongside them.

CHAPTER 26

Since he came to power in 1999, Oleg Butin dreamed of having men in the White House sympathetic to his desire to restore Russia's Imperial Might by conquering the independent Ukraine.

He found tacit support from America's Presidents Ali Hassan and later Duglas Trim. He hoped the conquest would lead him to fame in Russian historical annals comparable to Czar Peter and Stalin.

Shrouded in secrecy and deception, he prepared for an attack on Ukraine while he portrayed Russia as a democracy seemingly peaceful and tolerant of its neighbors.

He claimed Ukraine was not a country, only a region of Russia, and should not be a distinct State. In reality, his intent to conquer the country was far more sinister than an ordinary colonial land grab and enslavement of people.

His objective was to reclaim Ukraine's heritage and history as Russia's own by returning Ukraine to the anonymity it suffered at the hands of Peter the Great.

Ukraine was a separate country before Czar Peter defeated Hetman Mazepa at the battle of Poltava in 1709. By conquering Ukraine, Peter wanted his kingdom to become part of the European family of nations. He pretended his country originated from the seventh-century Ukrainian civilization rather than a remnant of the Mongol Empire in 1560.

He accomplished the deception after the conquest by renaming Muscovy in 1720 as Russia and declared it was the successor to Ukraine's ancient Kyivan Rus.

From then on, Ukraine ceased to exist as a distinct nation, and its history became Russia's own, except in the minds of the Ukrainian people, who clung to their identity despite three centuries of attempts to Russify them.

Ukrainians endured colonial anonymity, unable to rid themselves of the oppressive Russian yoke until they succeeded in bringing the downfall of the USSR.

Following the collapse of the Communist Empire in 1991, Moscow agreed to its borders with Ukraine. It acknowledged Ukraine's rightful share of the Soviet territory established as the Ukrainian SSR after the Second World War.

Recognizing Ukraine's sovereignty, presidents Maximov and Butin paid rent to Ukraine for leasing their naval base in Crimea. Moscow lived in peace with its democratic neighbor for 23 years.

Still, Oleg resented the peaceful arrangement because he believed the loss of Ukraine diminished Russia's Status as a Global Power.

After the fall of Communism, independent Ukraine became a nuclear Country, something the Kremlin wished to remove. Moscow gained support in NATO for removing Ukraine's nuclear arsenal.

The US, Britain, and France feared proliferation. They resolved to denuclearize Ukraine by guaranteeing its safety by signing the "Territorial Integrity of Ukraine" accord in exchange for its nuclear weapons.

The agreement made world headlines, but it rendered Ukraine defenseless, relying on the honesty of the signatories, including Russia, whose signature proved worthless.

The last nuclear delivery system left Ukraine in 2001. Oleg was already in charge and had no intention of honoring his country's commitment to Ukraine.

In 2008, he overcame the final hurdle in his quest to attack his neighbor. He kept Kyiv out of NATO by bribing the German Chancellor to block Ukraine from joining the organization in return for deep discounts on the price of Russian gas. Ukraine's membership in the defense pact would derail his conquest.

Butin

The arrangement was a financial one for Berlin's female leader. She grew up in East Germany during the years of communist occupation that brainwashed her to trust the Kremlin. Unfortunately, her decision spelled disaster for Ukrainians because it paved the way for Oleg's invasions.

Butin disregarded Russia's nuclear agreement and invaded Crimea after fomenting internal discourse in Ukraine in 2014. He threatened to nuke the other signatories if they intervened. The bluff worked wonders. Hassan did nothing tangible in response to the attack, letting Moscow annex the peninsula and occupy parts of Ukraine's Donbas.

The success of seizing the territory encouraged Oleg to embark on further conquest, which came in 2022 as a full-blown war against Ukraine with ferocity rivaling the German invasion of the country during WWII.

Butin pretended the reason for the conflict was to stop the persecution in Ukraine of the people whom the Kremlin labeled as Russian Speakers. He said they were loyal to Russia and would bring flowers to greet the invading troops as liberators.

To his dismay, the Ukrainians came out as one to defend their nation. They brought guns, not roses, to confront the invaders, proving the fake language issue was a lie.

The unity of Ukrainians should have been expected. Colonialism affected their speech, as elsewhere, but did not change their loyalty to their native land or nation. Once they gained independence, they united as no other nation and would never again submit to colonial occupation.

The West held its breath when Russians attacked, believing the fledgling democracy would collapse within a few days. It did not, and the fact infuriated Butin. He vowed in a tirade to his nation to wipe Ukrainians from the face of the Earth and erase Ukraine from the map of the world.

The invasion turned into a war rather than the expected rout. Oleg had to prepare Russians for a prolonged conflict against the stubborn resistance that began receiving weapons from the US.

Because Russia assaulted Orthodox Ukrainians who never harmed it, Oleg required more than the consent of the Russian Church and its Patriarch Onufry. He needed an incentive for the war that only blind hate could produce to make Russians attack their comrades in the Great Patriotic War.

To incite hatred, Moscow's disinformation factories labeled Ukrainian people as Nazis. The slogan transferred the loathing Russians had for Hitler's Germany to Ukraine. The propaganda lies, repeated a thousand times, became the call for war by the brainwashed Russian masses. They were convinced they were fighting fascists, not the democratic Ukrainians.

One might wonder how Russians could consider their previous compatriots as Nazis. To understand this absurdity, one should realize that the Kremlin used the closed press to condition the Russian people. In an Orwellian fashion, people were forced to accept lies as the truth and muzzle those who disagreed.

Russia's dishonesty about Ukrainians and its history began but did not end with Czar Peter. Each dictator that followed him embellished the deception with wishful scenarios. For instance, the czars referred to Ukrainians as "Little Russians" to diminish their identity.

The communists pretended Russians alone defeated Germany, ignoring the fact seven million Ukrainians served in the Soviet army and bore the brunt of the fight in Stalingrad.

Butin was no different from his predecessors. To vent his anger against the unyielding Ukrainians, he rewrote Russian history. He deleted any reference to Ukraine in its pages as though it never existed. It was what he wished, not a reality.

Like the stories about the Knights of the Round Table, past Russian historians invented a ninth-century Viking named Rurik as the founder of Kyivan Rus. However, no such character is mentioned anywhere in contemporary historical records. Serious scholars dismiss it as a fantasy.

In Butin's version of the fable, Rurik became the ruler of Rus with no mention of Kyiv.

CHAPTER 27

Before she departed, Father Semyon blessed her and said she should look out for an assassin that Butin would send to kill her. If they did not intend to murder her in the US, she would get orders to leave for Russia, where she would be imprisoned and tortured to reveal her contacts.

He knew that the FSB would make her confess that he was the go-between her and the FBI, so he asked the agency to change his identity and appearance and relocate him to a parish in Europe because he did not want to abandon the ministry of God.

The priest left her a one-time number if she needed to flee on short notice to escape assassination. The anonymous contact would arrange her getaway to Britain or the EU, where she could disappear under a new name.

A few days later, Efrem informed her that Onufry would replace her as his assistant, and she was to report to the embassy to return to Russia. She was being promoted to serve as an assistant to Russia's ecumenical representative in the Vatican.

Her replacement would arrive in three weeks. Before She left, she would introduce her replacement to Fallworth and the Council of the Christian Churches of America. Her replacement was two people, Father Maxim and nun Ludmila. Nadia immediately recognized the priest was Klimchuk and the assistant was Natasha, the daughter of Butin's childhood friend Irina.

She suspected the man was sent to assassinate her if that was their plan or accompany her back to Moscow and make sure she did not get away. The woman would take her place as the assistant to Onufry.

Her suspicion was quickly answered. A few days after he arrived, Maxim came to her quarters, pretending he was going there to hear her confession.

"Remember me, you bitch? I'm going to have some fun with you. I have been waiting for this since you embarrassed me in Kyiv in front of your hohol lover. The bastard was shot in the head when I pointed him out to the sniper squad leader."

"Relax, asshole, I'm not hard to get. We don't need to fight over it. I see, your tongue grew back, and your speech returned to normal.

Nadia began to undress as Klimchuk took off his cassock.

"Just one stipulation before we begin, there will be no kissing."

BUTIN

"Can I at least lick your tits?"

"Yes, but not on the mouth."

When he got on top of her and started to lick her breast, she reached under the pillow and jabbed him with a syringe.

"You bitch, what did you do he yelled as he grabbed her throat?"

"You'll sleep it off," she said as she heaved him off the bed.

She dressed in civilian clothing, went outside to a convenience store, and called a number on a disposable phone.

A disguised voice on the other end told her to wait on a street corner where she would be picked up within an hour by a cabby who would take her to a drop-off, from where she could walk to a specified address.

Dressed as a Muslim woman, she was on her way to France two weeks later as an employee of a French broadcasting agency. The news report said Bishop Efrem died of a massive brain hemorrhage. Nadia did not check in at the new workplace. She was going to Ukraine with Dmytro, a soup kitchen cook Orest introduced to her seven years ago.

Russia has just invaded Ukraine and marched on Kyiv with a huge tank convoy. Russia did to Ukraine what Hitler did to Ukraine for the same reason. A fascist land grab for the historical glory of its dictator. Russian propaganda referred to

Ukrainians as Nazis, but in reality, that is what the invading Russians were and did.

The world held its breath, waiting for the inevitable collapse of Ukraine everybody expected to occur within a day, except for Dmytro and Nadia. Both decided to become guerilla fighters if the Ukrainian army rejected them or the Ukrainian government sued for peace.

The army was happy to accept them as volunteers and assigned them to the same fighting unit. They were shown how to use shoulder-mounted anti-tank weapons and dispatched to confront the Russian tank convoy. There was no chaos because the army anticipated the invasion and was well organized to defend Kyiv against the overwhelming odds.

They were sent to the front of the invading tank column to destroy the leading tanks while another unit attacked the rear. The road was narrow, and the convoy was stalled, unable to move forward or retreat. The remaining tanks became sitting ducks for the defenders, who fought like an independent guerilla unit rather than a large army.

Nadia was tired but happy. She liked her partner. He was from Luhansk, a city in east Ukraine occupied by Russians in 2014.

BUTIN

He was in his late fifties and lost his son and wife in the first few days of the Russian assault on the city while he was still in Kyiv with the protesters.

They died in their house bombed by the false flag army of the warlord Igor. Dmytro felt guilty he was away at the time, but he would have died if he had not.

In Kyiv, he tried to save his friend Orest, who died in his arms. The death created his bond with Nadia. She was young enough to be his daughter, full of optimism as if she was reborn, free of her deadly profession.

ACKNOWLEDGEMENT

With gratitude to the refugees for their accounts of life under

tyranny.

ABOUT THE AUTHOR

Jason Wright is a former science teacher from Minnesota who has traveled extensively worldwide. He retired in Las Vegas as an author of political novels and murder mysteries.